Thai Breaker

Sinclair set his glass back down on the bar. The tapping returned, harder than before.

"Hey, maybe you don't hear so good, chalky. This is strictly yellow bar. No Westerners allowed."

Sinclair raised his glass as if to drink and, aiming for the owner of the voice, threw the contents over his shoulder.

Outraged curses answered.

Before they had a chance to react, he spun around on the bar stool and pummeled the nearest thug repeatedly in the stomach. Grunts of pain followed the steady thuds made by Sinclair's powerful fists hitting the soft belly of his potential attacker. When the man began to crumple, Sinclair sailed a hard right through his jaw that sent him and several teeth flying. He landed in a heap near the jukebox, and didn't think once about getting up.

Another one, short and wide, backed up a few paces and charged, head-first. This is just too easy, Sinclair thought. He waited until the man was almost upon him, then stepped coolly aside. The head barreled into the sturdy bar and followed the body to the floor. After a few shakes, its owner somehow rose to his feet, still bent over at the waist. Sinclair locked his hands together and, raising them high over his head, brought them crashing down on the back of the thick neck. This time it stayed where it was.

Breathing heavily and feeling more charged up than he could remember feeling in years, Sinclair turned to face the rest of the attack squad.

THE FORCE #1

DEADLY SNOW
by Jake Decker

PINNACLE BOOKS **NEW YORK**

THE FORCE #1: DEADLY SNOW

An original Pinnacle Books edition, published for the first time anywhere.

First printing, February 1984

ISBN: 0-523-42079-X

Can. ISBN: 0-523-43062-0

Cover illustration by Aleta Jenks

Printed in the United States of America

PINNACLE BOOKS, INC.
1430 Broadway
New York, New York 10018

9 8 7 6 5 4 3 2 1

Deadly Snow

prologue

The tall redhead slid her sunglasses down the bridge of her nose and peered over the top. She didn't see the two men anywhere.

Maybe she'd lost them. Maybe.

She looked at her watch: 12:40. The streets would be jammed with tourists, shoppers, workers taking lunch. A chance to make a break.

She walked warily through the revolving door of the Sakol Hotel and out into the sweltering Bangkok heat.

April was the peak of the Thai summer. Temperatures generally floated in the mid-nineties. Today was no exception. Women wore loose dresses or shorts and blouses, men thin cotton trousers and open-necked shirts.

She walked to the corner and bought a morning paper. Her picture was on the front page, bottom-right-hand corner. The headline said:

ACTRESS MISSING, FEARED DEAD

Under the picture: "Where is Tina Cooke? Story on page 5."

"Hey lady! Would ya mind movin'? You're blockin' the cash register."

Tina just stared at him, blankly.

"Hey! You okay?"

"Hmmm? Oh, yes, I'm fine, I'm fine." She smiled, tucked the newspaper under her arm, and began strolling down Rajadamnern Avenue, with no idea where she was going.

She entered the first dark restaurant she saw, the Bankeo Ruenkwan—"Authentic Thai cuisine. Major credit cards accepted"—and asked for a table near the back.

Before sitting down, she ordered the luncheon special, quickly flipped to page 5 of the newspaper. She sat in a chair facing the entrance of the small restaurant, and pulled the candle on her table close enough to read her obituary.

FILM STAR DISAPPEARS

April 6, Bangkok—Tina Cooke, sensuous starlet of more than half a dozen action-adventure films made in Thailand, is missing. Police report that the red-haired actress has not been seen for four days.

A spokesman for Dreamscape Films told reporters that Miss Cooke, 26, failed to show up for work on Tuesday, April 2. This did not arouse immediate suspicion, since the fiery actress is known for what the spokesman called "her fits of temperament."

Police were called in when Miss Cooke was again absent on Wednesday, April 3, and phone calls to her apartment failed to bring a response.

Lt. Juan Valjenos, Fight Coordinator for Dreamscape Films and a close friend of Miss Cooke, led police to her apartment, which was locked and bolted from the inside. A subsequent break-in by police revealed evidence of a burglary and/or assault.

Chairs and tables were overturned, various articles broken, several objects of value missing. Bloodstains on the rug and sofa matched Miss Cooke's own blood type, but no body was found.

Police speculate that . . .

"Excuse me, miss?"

Tina gasped, and looked up to see a waiter standing over her with a pot of tea and a plate of *gang pet*—pork curry.

"Pardon me for interrupting," he said coolly. "Could I set this down please?"

"Oh, yes, yes, of course." She folded the paper quickly and put it on her lap. As the waiter laid the meal out in front of her she tried to think of something logical to say. "I feel so silly for reacting that way. A . . . a friend of mine was in an accident. A car accident. I was just reading about it."

The waiter attempted a sympathetic smile. "Will there be anything else?"

"No." Why didn't he leave? "Thank you."

She watched until he was out of sight, then poured herself a cup of the strong black tea.

Its full-bodied pungence both awakened and calmed her. Now what, she asked herself, was going on?

Monday had been one of the most grueling and exhausting days Tina'd been through in her brief career as a "film star."

She had spent all day rehearsing her portion of the climactic fight scene in the new movie. It was the fourth in a series of films about the Circle of Eight martial-arts soldiers of fortune. She hadn't even spoken a line in the first two movies, but being the only occidental and the only woman made her conspicuous, and she attracted a lot of attention. In this film she even had lines in a few scenes and had made it up to fifth billing.

Tim Chang, the assistant fight coach who had blocked out this particular sequence, was very patient with her, but Tina feared she physically wasn't up to it. She was used to fighting segments of thirty seconds or a minute. At four minutes, this scene was designed to make her a major cult star. Or put her in a hospital. She'd been tense and snappish on the set for days.

Her partner for the fight, Sammy Wuan, was no help. Sammy had played second leads in several Chinese martial arts films in the early seventies. But drug arrests and clashes on the set caused him to be blacklisted. In '77 he quit pictures, or vice versa, and signed with a sports promotor as an exhibition fighter. For three years he toured Southeast Asia as the Hooded Horror and never "won" a match.

In 1980, while the circuit was playing Bangkok, he went to an open casting call and landed a job as a contract player with Dreamscape Films. His experience made him a natural for the new but blossoming movie industry in Thailand, where he hoped to rebuild his career.

A forlorn hope: at forty years old, five feet nine inches tall, 210 pounds and balding, he looked more like a Buddha than a Bruce Lee, but his skill combined with his appearance made Sammy the perfect screen villain.

Sammy resented Tina's newfound fame as much as her gender. He'd lost fights before, made his living losing them on the exhibition circuit. But always to a guy. He hated the idea of being beaten by a woman, even in a fictional contest.

The day was full of little "accidents," Sammy throwing Tina a little too hard, or coming a little too close to her with the blade of his prop machete, dull but potent enough to produce three or four angry purple bruises on Tina's arms by midafternoon.

Valjenos arrived at the rehearsal room around four, "Just to see how things are going."

Tina signaled for Sammy to stop. "Juan, I have to talk to you."

"Of course. What about?"

"In private."

He looked her straight in the eye, and said dryly, "Certainly. Sammy, Tim, take ten."

Tina heard Sammy snicker as he lumbered out the door.

Valjenos sat in the chair vacated by Tim Chang, put his feet up on the adjoining table, and said, "Now. What is the problem this time, Tina?"

"I want you to replace Sammy."

Valjenos said nothing, but stared at her impassively, dourly, like a psychiarist listening to the familiar ravings of a paranoid patient.

"Not fire him. Just get me a new partner for this sequence."

He began playing with a pencil he'd picked up from the table, twirling it between his hands, not taking his eyes off her.

"He's hurting me, Juan. Look at my arms. I think he's doing it on purpose." She paused and swallowed. "And I'm afraid of him."

"Good." Valjenos swung his feet off the table onto the floor and stood up. He spoke slowly and evenly. "Understand. That nothing goes on in this studio without my knowledge and consent. Perhaps Sammy was giving you a lesson ... or a warning. Remember, Miss Cooke, that you are not indispensable, either as an actress ... or as a person."

He cracked the pencil in two, and handed her the broken pieces. "You're through for the day. Your monthly check's waiting for you at the front office. If you don't want it to be your last, be on the set tomorrow at eight, sharp." He turned and walked crisply out of the room, leaving the door open behind him.

Tina walked home in a daze. Was Valjenos serious?

What could she do? For four years her life had revolved around her career. Strenuous physical training, long hours on the set, and homework left her little time for other interests. She had no friends outside the studio. Who could she turn to for help?

Instead of depositing her sizable paycheck, she cashed it and put all the bills in a side pocket of her purse. If she lost her job she could be on the very next plane out of Thailand. Maybe she'd visit her sister Jez in New York. Lots of aspiring actresses there.

After the strenuousness of the day, Tina decided to skip the evening workout and go straight from the bank to her apartment, where she could soak in a hot tub—for about a week.

The three-flight climb to her apartment door seemed to take an hour. She saw that she had again left the lights on. Absentminded as well as temperamental, she muttered to herself as she inserted the key in the lock.

"Never mind, Tina baby, it's open."

Sammy Wuan's voice. Furious, Tina kicked open the door. Sammy was sitting in her favorite chair, flanked by two men she had never seen before.

"Welcome home, dear. Hard day at the office?"

"What the hell are you doing here?"

"Cut the crap, baby." Sammy stood up. He held a knife. He stabbed the top of her coffee table with its sharp point. "You'll notice this is not a prop. You might call it an educational tool." The two men laughed silently, their shoulders shaking. "Because it'll teach you, and the world, not to poke around into the operation."

He held the knife out in front of him, and advanced on her, slowly.

Instinctively Tina crouched, began to breathe more heavily, and psyched herself into a state of deep concentration.

When Sammy was four feet in front of her she kicked up with all her strength, hitting him squarely in the balls. He screamed in pain and fell to the floor, clutching himself. The knife lay on the carpet in front of him.

She leaped on the weapon like a ravenous cat attacking a mouse and lifted it high over her head. She plunged the blade deep into the warm flesh of the man writhing on the floor in front of her. Her anger and outrage from the day boiling over, she stabbed again and again and again, oblivious to Sammy's agonized squeals. Dark red life gushed out of his body onto the floor, her arms, her clothes. Sammy's two accomplices stood motionless, shocked into paralysis by the bestial display.

The knife slipped out of Tina's sweaty hands. She looked into the pool of blood where it had fallen. Her whiplash fury turned to revulsion as the enormity of her act struck her. She stumbled, horrified, out the doorway, her eyes never leaving the scene.

Sammy's squeals of pain followed her as she ran down the hallway, echoed in her mind long after she was down the stairs, out the street door, and wandering the dark Bangkok night.

She roamed the streets for hours, ending up in Chinatown.

Chinatown was Bangkok's crime hub, at night a festival of drugs, prostitution, and assaults of all varieties. Tourists or strangers who ventured there after dark invariably regretted the trip.

But no one bothered the tall red-haired girl. Anyone could see by the way she walked that she was high as a kite. Undoubtedly a prostitute. And the stains on her clothes probably meant she'd just had a fight with her pimp. Hands off.

Tina checked into the Sakol Hotel, once a plush four-star accommodation, now a fleabag catering mostly to girls and their guests for an hour or two.

She slept for two days.

She woke Thursday, in the middle of the night, took a long hot bath, and tried to put the pieces together.

Running over Monday's events in her mind led nowhere. It just didn't add up, no matter how many times she went through it.

Maybe if she wrote it down.

The only paper in her purse was a half-finished letter to her sister. She pulled it out and laid it on the bed in front of her. The third page was practically blank. Tina wrote out everything she remembered about Monday, from the rehearsal to Valjenos's "advice" to the attack in her apartment.

She was reading over her account for the umpteenth time when a soft knock on the door interrupted her.

"Who is it?"

"Li. I mean, the maid." The voice, a young girl's, faltered. "I . . . I'm here to clean the room."

"Just a minute." Tina wrapped a bedspread around her naked body. "Come in."

The door opened slowly and a thin Thai girl wearing jeans and a halter top tiptoed in. About twelve, Tina judged.

The girl approached the bed timidly. "I have fresh linen and towels."

"Good for you." Tina stretched and, picking up the letter, crossed to the window. "What time is it . . ." She searched her brain for the girl's name, finally giving up. "What did you say your name was?"

"Li. About four-thirty."

"Mm." Tina looked around at the street below. Should she wait until dark and make a break? She looked down at the bedspread she wore and remembered her bloodstained clothes. Call someone for help? Go to the police? A picture of Sammy lying dead on the floor flashed through her brain. No.

Then she saw them. Sammy's two friends. Just waiting.

"Listen, Li, there's an errand I'd like you to run

for me." She grabbed her purse and pulled out the wad of bills she'd gotten on Monday.

Li's eyes widened at the sight of the money. "What do you want me to do?"

Tina peeled off five one-hundred-baht bills and pressed them into the girl's hand. "Buy me a dress, size eight, and a wristwatch, an inexpensive one, and a pair of sunglasses."

"Anything you say, Miss Cooke."

Tina stared at her in disbelief. "You know who I am?"

Li nodded slowly.

Tina peeled off two more bills. "Give this one to the desk clerk, and keep this one for yourself."

Li stuffed the bills in her pocket and bounded out of the room.

Tina settled down into a chair near the window and waited.

She must have fallen asleep, for the next thing she remembered was bright sunlight glaring into her eyes. She was still in the chair, and in the bedspread.

There was no sign of Li, but laid out neatly on the bed were a yellow summer dress, a pair of sunglasses, and a wristwatch.

She put on all three. The watch was running. The time: 12:23.

Thank you, Li.

She left another bill on the bed, picked up her purse, and walked down the stairs to face whatever lay ahead.

Tina poured out another cup of tea.

Why hadn't they found Sammy's body? Maybe they had. Were the police seeking her as victim or killer?

"Excuse me, miss." That fucking waiter again. "The gentleman at the bar would like to join you. He says you're expecting him."

She looked over, and there was Valjenos, not twenty feet away.

"Oh, dear." She tried to sound annoyed rather than terrified. "That's my ex-husband." She pulled a bill from her purse and laid it on the table. "Is there a back way out of here?"

The waiter pocketed the bill. "Down the hallway to your right, second door on the right."

"Thanks."

Tina and the waiter left the table simultaneously. He went to the bar and received three five-hundred-baht bills and a small white packet from Valjenos. She went out the back door and received three .22-caliber bullets and a horizontal slash across the throat.

A few blocks away, a little girl was mailing a letter she found on a windowsill in Room 317 of the Sakol Hotel.

chapter 1

Space boots.

Carefully, Micah locked his feet and ankles into the molded plastic boots so that his toes wiggled freely. The boots were well padded on the inside and were completely comfortable, despite the fact that their appearance suggested some futuristic inquisition.

Satisfied with the quality of his purchase, Micah anchored both hands onto the overhead tracking he'd recently installed and, swinging his body upward, locked the boots onto the track.

Exhaling, he slowly relaxed every muscle, till he hung, fully inverted from the ceiling track, naked save for a pair of gym shorts. Hands clasped behind his head, Micah began a series of involved calisthenics, not breaking his concentration, even when the door to his studio apartment was flung open.

"Oh, wow." Nineteen-year-old Patty Farrell, pretty, blond hair to her belly button, not overburdened with intelligence, walked through the door carrying a filled laundry basket. Her round, child-like eyes fixed on the apparatus Micah hung from.

"These are, y'know, furnished apartments." A frown creased her features. "You're not supposed to put stuff on the ceiling, you're not even supposed to hang pictures! Mrs. Digs will have heart failure."

With a sudden lunge, Micah freed himself from the track, landing on his feet lightly. "Mrs. Digs's heart is very sound, Patty," he chided, stepping out of the boots.

"I told you not to call me that." One pink hand flipped blond strands from her shoulder. "Patricia is, like, my mother's idea of a name. I want you to call me Earthworm; I feel it expresses my being." She watched him pull a bathrobe over his smooth muscles.

"Got my laundry?" He padded on bare feet to the refrigerator, inspecting its meager contents while she sifted through the laundry basket.

"Yeah." She looked up as he swung the refrigerator door shut. "Y'know, Micah, I was thinking." She shrugged, round shoulders rising and falling like a heartbeat. "Maybe if you're around, we could go white-water rafting next weekend."

He smiled. "It's difficult for me to make plans for the future."

"Right." Nodding wisely, she rose, clutching her basket as she headed for the door. "See you."

"See you."

Remembrance struck her, and she turned back to him, one finger held up, sporting an imaginary string. "I almost forgot. I thought I was tripping in the laundry room. Some guy dressed like a narc told me to tell you that you have an overdue library book." She pouted, an affectation for some, a natural gesture for Patty/Earthworm. "Does that make any sense to you."

Micah's smile faded. With easy strides he covered the distance between his previous location and her present one. "Perfect sense."

"Oh." Her tone implied an understanding her bewildered eyes belied. "No white-water rafting huh?"

" 'Fraid not." He sighed. "You'd better tell Mrs. Digs my rooms are to let." He leaned forward and kissed her lightly on the forehead.

He would have kissed her on the lips, but you never knew where a girl named Earthworm might have been last.

*   *   *

"Can I help you?" Firmly ensconced behind a massive desk, the sensibly dressed young woman exuded authority . . . and that was all she exuded, Micah noted sourly.

The slate-topped desk came up to the leather-patched elbows of her tweed jacket.

Keeping his voice at the low level proper for the library, Micah leaned forward. He knew, from his vast and varied background, that most North Americans preferred a sphere of some three-to-four feet between themselves and new acquaintances. Micah was Cajun and New Orleans had never considered itself quite like the rest of North America. He leaned forward, knowing she would flinch back. She did.

Typical, he surmised, drumming lean brown fingers on the desk top. "I understand you have a reference book on reserve for me. My name is Micah."

"So you're Micah." Gracefully, she slipped from

the swivel chair. "I must say I've been quite curious about you ever since I read your dossier."

"Oh? I'd always assumed my dossier was classified."

She stood before him now, a very neat 115 pounds on two very nice legs. "I am classified, Micah." She grasped his hand in a businesslike manner. He held on a second longer than was customary, watching a slow blush creep up to her hairline. She really was pretty, Micah decided, particularly when she was confused.

Motioning for him to follow, she started toward the freight elevator. "I've never seen you here before, but your dossier said you'd been with the Association for six years."

After he'd stepped into the elevator, she pushed the red button marked "alarm." No alarm sounded as the car descended noiselessly.

"I've always received my assignments through Charles Davis," Micah explained. "Guess that's why I'm a little surprised to be summoned into the great man's presence. How is Charlie? Haven't heard a word from him."

"Charles Davis is retired." She answered quickly. "The Librarian has authorized me to advise you of Davis's present status."

Micah whistled softly. "From the great man himself."

"That's right." A cushioned shock announced the end of the elevator's journey.

She stepped out and continued down the corridor, stopping at a utility closet.

"In there?" A quick inspection told Micah that the utility closet was precisely that. The small, windowless room housed a variety of mops and pails, all showing the advanced stages of age and disuse. A window pole was propped up in one corner. He turned around, quickly scanning.

"Perhaps you've made a mistake." She was suddenly absorbed in the study of a loose thread on her jacket sleeve.

Wait a minute, Micah thought. A window pole in a room with no windows? Not a speck of dust on it either. Grasping the slim rod, he tapped at the ceiling tiles. The sixth tile gave. Another tap dislodged the panel completely, leaving a gaping black hole in the ceiling.

On impulse, he twisted the pole. He felt something catch on the hook at the end of the pole. Pulling downward, a cord, like an old-fashioned bell pull fell into the closet. A note was attached. Another good pull and the whole closet began to descend; the damn thing was another elevator.

He opened the note. *Very good, Micah*, it read.

The young Cajun threw back his head and howled with laughter. "Why does he do these things?"

The woman smiled. "I suppose it's to keep us on our toes. Unless, of course, this is his idea of fun. You should see what I go through just to deliver his coffee and Danish in the morning."

The wall of the pseudo-utility closet slid back into a concealed panel, revealing the comfortable English-style study of the Librarian ... and the Librarian himself.

He rose from his easy chair to greet Micah and his guide.

"Thank you, Pamela, for making sure our honored guest arrived ... uneventfully. Micah ..." The Librarian offered his hand, which Micah clasped respectfully.

"How are you, sir? It's been quite a while."

"Five years." The Librarian answered precisely. "You were just twenty, I believe." He ushered Micah to a chair. Pamela perched on the desk.

"Going to take notes?" Micah inquired brightly.

"No need." The Librarian waved a careless hand. "Pamela has a photographic memory." Seeing Micah regard the young woman with new respect, he added, "Also, perfect pitch." Pamela nodded an assent.

"But, you must wonder," the Librarian continued, "why I've arranged this meeting instead of going through the usual channels."

Micah shrugged. "I suppose it's because Charlie Davis is dead."

Pamela stifled an involuntary cry. "I never said—"

"You didn't have to." Micah smiled. She really did have great legs. "Your heartbeat altered substantially when you told me about Charlie. You felt stress because you assumed Charlie and I were friends. We weren't, just co-workers."

"But no one can hear a heartbeat," she blurted. "That's impossible!"

"Impossible, no." Micah frowned. "Just very, very difficult."

"You see, Pamela? Our Micah is quite a gifted man." The Librarian folded his hands, a gesture Micah recognized as a prelude to the crux of this meeting. On cue, Pamela set a bulky folder in front of Micah, then returned to the desk.

"What do you know of Thailand, Micah?"

"White elephants." Again, the Cajun shrugged. "Oh yes, they shot *The Bridge on the River Kwai* there."

"They also make heroin there. Oh, not the Thais. Outside of an occasional pipeful, they don't seem to have much use for the stuff. But there are other, outside groups, much to the Thai government's chagrin, that are running drugs from the secret poppy fields in the northern part of the country to every reach of the civilized world. We have reasons to believe Lord D'Arbanville is involved."

"D'Arbanville." Micah couldn't say he was surprised. After he'd bought his title from an impoverished English noble, Richard D'Arbanville had become infamous as the leader of an international crime ring. D'Arbanville had always been a white slaver. Now he was branching out into drugs. The old Fail-Safe Force had tangled with D'Arbanville a number of times, but as Micah knew from recent Association dispatches, The F.S. Force had all been killed, save for Steven Sinclair. . . .

"Lately D'Arbanville's been financing a film production company, Dreamscape Films," the Librarian continued. "Kung-fu movies and the like. At first we thought it was a money-laundering operation, but now we're quite sure he's using the company to establish drug pickup sites with his distributors."

"Do you know how?"

"Of course not, Micah. We have to leave something for our operatives to figure out."

Micah opened the folder Pamela had provided. The face of a beautiful girl stared up at him.

"One of D'Arbanville's people?"

The Librarian shook his head. "An actress employed by Dreamscape. She must have heard or seen something she shouldn't have, because the poor girl met a rather mysterious demise. Her sister is quite concerned; when we contacted her, she proved most cooperative. Apparently, the slain actress was quite a correspondent. There are a lot of letters, things of that nature."

Among the papers in the folder, Micah found a sheet on one Jezebel Cooke. The sister. There was no picture. He closed the folder.

"Fine. Then I'm ready to go. I understand Thai Airlines is wonderfully hospitable."

"This is not a solo operation. You cannot go alone." The Librarian leaned forward. "Do not make the mistake of underestimating D'Arbanville. You know what happened to the old Fail-Safe Force."

"Sinclair's still alive. Send him with me."

"Sinclair is no longer operative," Pamela interjected. "He's retired." Remembering Micah's unusual talents, she added, "Honest!"

"We will decide who is to accompany you to Thailand." The Librarian ushered Micah to the door. "Study the file. And when you approach Miss Cooke, please use a little more tact than you did with Pamela."

Micah grimaced. "Will do."

"Oh, yes. Micah? *The Bridge on the River Kwai* was filmed in Ceylon, not Thailand." A brief smile flickered across the Librarian's somber features. "Just thought you'd like to know."

*   *   *

Pamela flipped buttons, activating and deactivating the closed-circuit TV monitors the Librarian had installed throughout the library. Hallways, lavatories, closets, All clear.

"He's gone," she informed the Librarian.

"Well, what do you think of him?" Seeing her reluctance to pass judgments, he added, "Cocky little bastard, isn't he?"

"But, sir," Pamela argued. "I've studied his file. It's incredible. Every mission a success, accepted into the Association as a full operative at the age of nineteen. And his skills! Besides a solid background in computers and electronics, he's a master of weaponry, including fencing and Kendo."

"And he's a mental dominant."

Pamela looked surprised. That bit of information was not in the files.

The Librarian explained. "It's rather like snake charming, except you do it with people. So, Pamela, what is wrong with this extraordinary young man?"

"I don't know," she fished lamely.

"Check the personal bio," he prompted.

"He's had a . . . difficult life." An understatement, if the terse lines in the file were not a morbid fiction. "Orphaned young, quite a loner." She looked up hopefully. "Is that it?"

"Partly. He's an excellent agent, but Micah chose this field of endeavor because he enjoys the game. No family ties, no loyalty based on religious or cultural groups. Never had a partner. He fights for the joy of fighting. So reason with me, Pamela. If he plays because he enjoys the game, at what point will he cease to care what team he plays for?"

Pamela nodded in understanding. "What can the Association do, though? Resurrect the family Micah lost?"

"To some degree. I had hoped to phase him into the old Fail-Safe Force, but of course that is now impossible. But I can give him a partner. Someone smarter, more experienced, someone who can gain his respect, and through that, his allegiance."

"Sinclair."

"Sinclair."

Pamela frowned. "He's retired. I remember the dispatch he sent you. 'Course I remember all the dispatches. This one went: 'I'm fed up with the whole damn—' "

"He's the only man for the job," the Librarian interjected. He indicated the phone. "Ring up Ma's Diner. Let's see if we can change Mr. Sinclair's mind."

chapter 2

Ma looked up from his copy of *Playboy* with real annoyance. "If somebody don't pick up that blankety-blank phone, I'm gonna pull it off the blankety-blank wall!" He did not believe in using profanity in front of women, namely his two waitresses, Ruby and Lucille. At night there was a succession of high school girls, cute enough to keep the truckers smiling into their java; those kids just didn't give a hoot about the diner business.

Ma'd been pushing sixty halfway to Tuscon. His hair was white and his eyes held a trace of blue in the whites, like a little kid's. It was hard to imagine he had a record of twenty-one hard-earned kills. That was a big laugh around the Association; he'd tied Billy the Kid's record.

Ma had come in, put his past aside. Per standard procedure, the Association had issued him a new identity: one Harv Lipscomb, but anyone who'd ever traveled Route 54 knew him as Ma, of Ma's Diner fame.

It was one of the few places left where you could

still get a cold beer and a really good burger. Not to mention the chance to ogle a real live waitress.

Ruby was a Clairol redhead and Lucille a peroxide blond. They both smelled strongly of Angel-Face powder. Nobody complained.

Ma knew Lucille was just a divorced lady who enjoyed the extra cash and the truckers' flattery; he wondered about Ruby. The Association farmed out a lot of old operatives.

Ruby answered the blankety-blank phone; she usually did.

The man sitting at the counter, across from Ma, looked up. With no pretense of nonchalance, he watched Ruby at the phone. The beehive hairdo waggled as she responded to the unseen voice at the other end of the line. Unconscious of the weight of three coats of mascara plus eyeliner, her eyes flicked around the diner restlessly. Finally, they were drawn to *him*.

The man at the counter.

Ruby tapped the receiver with an overlong fingernail; they were false and it took her an hour to get them on straight, but they were worth the effort. Her eyebrows shot up quizzically; the man at the counter was nodding a slow negative. She hung up the phone. As an afterthought, she checked the coin return.

Now, what the hell was all that about, Ma wondered, temporarily distracted from Miss April's charms.

Ruby ambled over to the counter with her flat-footed waitress's gait. "Refill, Mr. Sinclair?"

Gratefully, the man at the counter handed his cup to that redheaded wonder named Ruby. Tucked between cup and saucer was a neatly folded fifty-dollar bill. "Thanks, Ruby."

She shrugged. "Aw, you don't have to do that," she said, pocketing the bill. "You want to duck a phone call from your boss, it's no skin off my nose." The coffeepot hissed as she set it back on the warmer. "I just never would have figured you worked in a library."

Lucille called over. "Hey, Red, you still working here?" There was just a trace of jealousy in her voice. Seemed every time Ma's buddy, Ma's handsome, gray-eyed buddy, was around, Ruby made sure she waited on him.

"Coming!" the redhead yelped.

Ma, thoughtfully tapping on Miss April's left breast, watched Ruby's retreating back. "I thought you had . . . retired."

Steve Sinclair stared into the muddy depths of his coffee cup. "I have."

He had, too. He'd had his fill of playing guardian of Western civilization. It was a bloody, destructive game he'd given his all to, and his all had been snapped up pretty quickly. He'd given up any chance he could possibly have had of future happiness. For a brief second, he indulged himself, allowed himself to remember a fleeting honey-blond sweetness, green eyes . . .

"Hey!" Ma rescued the coffee cup before it hit. The coffee was another story. Ruefully, he reached for the mop stashed behind the counter. "You got to relax, Steve. You're out of it, now."

Instinctively, Sinclair's strong hands balled into fists. Dangerous-looking fists. "They keep calling me."

"Damn, that's a tough one," Ma commiserated.

Deep inside, though, he was perplexed. There had been no phone calls after he himself had retired. Why was the Association still hounding Steve Sinclair?

A group of truckers was heading for the door, leaving behind a mountain of debris on table six. Lemon-meringue remains next to empty packets of Sweet and Low. The lunch rush, such as it was, was over. Ma's Diner was pretty quiet. Just Ma flipping through *Playboy*, Lucille and Ruby comparing lipstick shades, Steve Sinclair contemplating an empty cup.

So when Micah entered, he might as well have been leading a big brass band, all stark naked, the way they all stared at him. Only Sinclair chose to break the silence, with soft laughter. He could smell an Association man a mile away. Apparently the Librarian was no longer content with phone calls.

Ma turned to his two waitresses. "Good time to clean up the storeroom, ladies." Without their customary complaints, Ruby and Lucille discreetly vanished. Ma hunkered over the counter, waiting for the fireworks. He, too, knew an Association man by sight.

"So." Sinclair leaned back easily. "You're the Librarian's new errand boy."

Thinly veiled anger flashed across Micah's face. Bet he goes up like dry tinder, Ma thought.

The anger was replaced by a slow smile. "So, you're the burnout case. I'd recognize you anywhere, Sinclair."

Ma snarled. "You better watch your step, sonny. This man can take you apart and reassemble you as a whole new species."

Micah's smile grew wider. "But those days are gone, aren't they, Stevie?" He eased his body onto the stool next to Sinclair's. "The Librarian's all upset his prize boy turned chickenshit. Now, me . . . I'm just curious. Did you run out of luck . . . or balls?"

"F'God's sakes, Steve!" Ma burst out. "Rip the kid apart already!"

Now it was Sinclair's turn to smile. "Now, now, Ma, let's not be unhospitable. Get the kid a beer."

Grumbling, Ma complied. They all became engrossed in watching the rich head peep above the glass.

"Well, kid." Sinclair handed him the glass, still smiling coolly, "that is the baldest job of baiting I have ever been subjected to. Is there something on your mind, or are you just anxious to lose your teeth?"

"I bet there are guys standing in line to take a poke at you," Ma put in.

Micah sipped at his beer. "A few ladies, too."

In the storeroom, Ruby and Lucille cackled. Little pitchers have big ears. Well, not such little pitchers.

Sinclair was beginning to get tired of this particular game. He wasn't going to waste his time playing footsie with some hotshot Association whiz kid.

Almost as if he had been reading Sinclair's mind, Micah changed tactics. "Look, I've enjoyed fencing with you, Mr. Sinclair . . ." The "mister" did not escape Sinclair's notice. Gee, Mr. Sinclair, I'm sorry I was such a brat. Can we talk like grown-ups, now? "But I did come here to discuss something with you."

"No you didn't." He reached behind the counter and got himself a cold one. "You came here to give me a little song and dance about how the old team needs me, how the world can't spin without guys like you and me spilling our blood to keep the people of the free world safe." Except the ones standing too close to us, he amended silently. They get caught in the crossfire.

"I look lousy in a cheerleader skirt. Let me level with you."

"Please," Sinclair interjected drily.

"The Librarian's assigned me to a particularly interesting mission in Thailand. Narcotics. Normally, I'd be on the job an hour after the dossier was in my hands, but the Librarian won't let me fly solo. Guess he's worried I'll lose my teeth." Micah smiled broadly. It really would be a shame if those teeth wound up on somebody's floor. "I want this mission, Sinclair. But I'm not going to wet-nurse some improvised team that the Librarian's hand-picked to baby-sit me. I won't work with anyone who isn't equal to my skills."

"What about superior?"

"Are you?" Again, the challenge. The idea of outfitting Micah with a full set of dentures was becoming more and more appealing. "The Librarian thinks so. He thinks I could learn a few things from you." His eyes were serious and thoughtful. "Now, I'm not adverse to that; I've called a few men teacher in my day. But they've been damn fine men. I haven't seen anything yet that tells me you're not used up and washed up. Except the Librarian's word. So what does that leave me? One big question mark. Just what are you, Mr. Sinclair?"

Steve chucked the empty beer bottle in a wide arc. It sailed past Ma's ear and landed in the garbage bin. He turned back to Micah. "I am on vacation, of the permanent variety. I do not get involved anymore in the problems of the free world . . . and we have nothing left to talk about, Mr. . . ."

"Micah."

"Micah . . . ?" Sinclair fished.

"Just Micah." Again that sudden flash of anger. Micah no-name didn't like to answer questions, just ask them.

"You'd better go back to the library, pick out the first string."

Micah cocked his head to one side, the pose of the eternal bad boy. "Won't be like the old F.S. Force. That's a dying breed."

Moving so quickly he barely disturbed the dust motes floating in the still air, Sinclair left his seat at the counter and did not slow his momentum until he was toe to toe with Micah. He had two nice fistfuls of the Cajun's collar. "Let's have a little respect for the dead, shall we?" He muttered between clenched teeth. "Unless you'd care to join the ranks."

"Careful, you're messing the suit." Micah was unperturbed.

Slowly, Sinclair let go.

"I've read your file." Micah called over his shoulder as he headed for the door. "You'd never hurt one of the good guys."

Ma watched him get into his car through the wide front window. It was a little sports job, flashy. Good pickup, too, Ma noted as the car peeled out. "If that's what the good guys have come to, it's time to join the other side." The ex-agent shook his head in disgust. He dipped his hand into the ice-filled bin and hauled out two more cold bottles, tossing one to Sinclair.

"Ma?"

"Hmmm?" He let one hand dangle in the ice; this day sure was hotting up.

"Why did you retire?"

Ma shrugged. "Too old, getting too slow. I just knew if I went out on one more mission, they'd be sending me home in a baggie, and I sure ain't no Spartan. I plan to die in bed, with my arms around Ruby or Lucille. Hell, both of 'em, if I can manage."

More gleeful cackles erupted from the storeroom. "Figure that's why everyone retires," Ma summed up.

Steve closed his eyes reflectively. He didn't feel slower. Micah no-name sure didn't think Steve Sinclair had slowed up any. It was something else that was missing. Motivation, maybe. Whatever it was, it was gone, and Sinclair knew another mission could be suicide. And he wasn't that crazy.

"Oh, shit," Ma remarked conversationally. "Dragon's Teeth."

He stared out the window. A pack of motorcycles was roaring up Route 54, kicking up enough dust to hide a Cessna in. "Local assholes," Ma explained to Sinclair. "Dumb, but you don't need a college degree to bust things up. I better evacuate the ladies." In the storeroom, the waitresses scampered like frightened mice.

Gray eyes narrowed. "Don't bother, Ma. Think I'll go out and chat with the nice boys." The screen door slammed behind him, as the hot air closed in, carrying the smell of motorcycle exhaust. "Eleven punks. I hate uneven numbers."

Sinclair craned his neck sharp left. Micah lounged against the side of the diner. He'd removed his jacket and rolled up his sleeves. "I just pulled my car around the back. Heard these guys coming a mile away. Thought you might want some company."

"Suit yourself." He leaned against the diner, eyes heavy-lidded against the sun. The cyclists were all assembled now, their gleaming bikes lined up like Lippizan stallions. Silently they grouped, a sea of dirty leather vests surging forward, chains swinging against grimy jeans.

Sinclair easily identified the leader; the wit had a tattoo of a dragon's head on one beefy biceps. The dragon was munching on a naked woman. Whenever the biker flexed, the dragon took another bite.

The head biker paused in front of Sinclair. "Hey, man, you're in my way." His breath was like old salami. "My pals and I just want to get a few brews. Maybe talk to the nice ladies inside."

"I'm sure the ladies wouldn't mind if you all scooted home for a quick shower and a shave."

"Shit"—the biker laughed unpleasantly—"those old porkers should kiss our . . . feet, for giving them some." The gang laughed raucously.

Sinclair tensed, ready to spring at the first move. He felt the Cajun's hand on his shoulder. Micah faced the tattooed biker. The biker had a solid forty pounds on him.

Okay, smart-ass, let's see you handle this, Sinclair thought.

"Your shoelace is untied."

Sinclair groaned, but Micah's grin never wavered. Then, unbelievably, the biker looked down at his feet, his dirty sandal-clad feet. He was still staring down at those nonexistent shoelaces when Micah dealt him a very precise, very nasty karate chop to the back of the neck. The biker dropped like a sack of potatoes.

The next wave advanced menacingly. "Look." A man Sinclair assumed was the second in command pointed an accusing finger. "I don't care what sort of trick that was, peckerwood, you better not try that shit with me."

As the last word left his mouth he charged, propelling his bulky frame forward. Buckling his knees, Micah slipped down and around the biker's headlong rush, watching the hammy fists crash into the wall, splinters flying. A ragged howl sounded, as he stuffed his broken knuckles under his armpits.

Micah turned to Sinclair. "Your turn," he said brightly.

Thanks a lot, Sinclair thought. He was a little out of practice for this kind of sport, but instinctively he crouched, body perfectly balanced over his knees, gray eyes searching the faces of his opponents. Any move a man makes he's made in his head long before the message gets to his body.

One greasy-headed punk reached inside his leather vest. Sinclair saw the flicker in his eyes and, arcing his body around, slammed a heavy boot into the kid's wrist. Screaming, the punk dropped the knife and Sinclair followed through the momentum of his kick, shattering the blade beneath his heel.

A rough forearm snaked out from behind him, around his neck, crushing his windpipe. Another biker closed in, thudding his fists into Sinclair's stomach. A brief thought flashed through Sinclair's head, where was that smart-ass Association kid, now? He tensed his abdominal muscles; the punches still hurt, but he wasn't going to lose his lunch over it.

He grabbed the suffocating arm at the elbow and wrist and, turning his head sideways, slipped out of the choke-hold. Keeping his grip on the wrist, he ducked behind the choker and yanked up. With a barely audible crunch, cartilage gave way as shoulder and arm separated.

It was a satisfying sound. Sinclair hated anyone who'd hold a man down while his buddies pounded on him like rock at the meat packers. You get what you give.

A Dragon's Teeth member, swinging a sawed-off pool cue, lunged at him. Before Sinclair could react, Micah grabbed the cue as it swung by. A quick twist wrenched the cue away and Micah put it to good use, rapping it smartly on the biker's kneecaps. The biker joined his pals, howling in agony as they rolled in the dust of Ma's parking lot.

"What took you so long?" Sinclair gasped, as he tossed a biker into the path of Micah's pool cue.

"Just watching you, Sinclair. Poetry, man. Absolute Shakespeare."

He shifted, letting Sinclair's pitch thud helplessly against the diner. More splinters erupted. Micah was unconcerned. A little paint and putty would fix that up just fine.

The two agents faced off, each taking two gang members. Micah dispatched his quickly. He let the first man rush him, knocking him down. The biker never counted on the variation of a standard judo move Micah handed him. The Cajun fell onto his back, pulling his assailant with him, but instead of flipping the biker with his feet planted on the man's stomach, Micah opted for a lower target. Clutching his groin, the biker slammed against his pal. They both fetched up against the side of the diner. More splinters.

Sinclair elected a different approach. Something in his eyes changed, clicked into a different, higher gear. One of his prey turned tail and ran. He eyed the remaining Dragon's Tooth.

"You want to buy out like your buddy?" he asked softly.

In answer, the biker rushed forward, throwing a strong right to Sinclair's jaw. He blocked and jabbed at the biker's midsection: not killing blows, almost teasing.

He doesn't want it to end, Micah realized. He's enjoying it.

He was. Dancing lightly on his toes, Steve Sinclair hadn't felt so aware, so alive since . . . for a long time. He blocked and parried, till the biker was crying out of frustration and pain, blubbering like the big baby he was. Taking pity, Sinclair stepped in, striking him sharply on the jaw. The biker collapsed like a house of cards.

Sinclair grabbed the gang leader by the collar, muttering to Micah, "I wondered if you'd gone out for a pizza after you took out Tattoo."

The Cajun laughed. "You think it's easy convincing a guy wearing sandals that his shoelaces are untied? Takes a little effort."

"Then you should have timed your party trick a little later." He shook the Dragon's Tooth, until he came to. "I think you have an apology to make. Ruby! Lucille!"

Ma and the two waitresses came to the screen

door. It was hanging drunkenly from one hinge. No one looked terribly surprised.

Sinclair shook the biker till his vertebrae rattled. "C'mon, make it sincere."

"Sorry." He mumbled. Then as Sinclair's thumb bore down on the nerve center at the junction of neck and shoulder, he shrieked, "I'm sorry!" with great sincerity.

Sinclair sent him sprawling in the dust. "If you ever bother these ladies again, or show up on these premises, you better grow eyes in the back of your head so you can watch out for me." Steve Sinclair was also capable of great sincerity.

The vanquished Dragon's Teeth started picking up their wounded and crawling back to their bikes.

chapter 3

"Nice going, hotshot." Sinclair executed a courtly bow and, holding what was left of the door open, gestured slowly toward the debris outside of Ma's Diner.

Micah tried not to laugh as he crossed back into the greasy spoon.

"Looks better'n it did before them smelly gorillas busted in here," Lucille chimed in.

As they settled back into a booth Micah shrugged, looked thoughtfully at Sinclair, and said, "I see what you mean about not getting involved."

Sinclair's smile faded. "I make an exception occasionally with my friends."

"How about enemies? We think that someone you . . . know is behind the operation."

The sound of breaking glass caused both men to shift their attention to behind the counter.

"Guess my hand musta slipped," Ma said in a very small voice. "They just don't make beer bottles like they used to."

Sinclair grinned in spite of himself. "Ma, is it all right if we use the office?"

"Uh, sure thing, Steve," Ma said. The two men got up and walked toward an orange door marked "private." "I'll just take care of this mess." They entered the small office and closed the door. "Sort of hold down the fort."

Ma's office was also his bedroom. It contained a cot, lamp, card table, two chairs, and about a year's worth of old newspapers.

As soon as the door was closed Sinclair demanded, "All right. Who is it?"

Micah considered withholding the name until he had relaxed Sinclair a little, but the determination in the older man's steel-gray eyes caused him to abandon that plan. He said simply, "D'Arbanville."

"He's dead." Sinclair almost spat out the words. The effect was like an explosion. His bottled rage flashed momentarily, and just as suddenly evaporated into stillness.

Micah let the postfury silence settle over the two of them before proceeding. He sat in one of the room's two chairs and motioned Sinclair into the other. "So we thought." He produced a large gray envelope from his inside jacket. "A man fitting D'Arbanville's description surfaced in Canberra last year. He used the name George Wembley."

"So?"

"So Wembley is D'Arbanville's mother's maiden name."

"Sentimental bastard."

"Mm. Wembley's modus operandi corresponded to the pattern you outlined in your report on D'Arbanville's activities in Scotland and England."

Sinclair frowned. "Pretty flimsy evidence."

Micah could see they were at a stalemate. He looked down at the gray envelope he held tightly in his left hand. His trump card. Should he play it or wait for Sinclair to come over on his own?

Suddenly Sinclair pushed his chair back and headed for the door. Micah knew he had no choice. "There's more."

Sinclair's fingers fell away from the doorknob. "What?"

As Micah slowly unclasped and opened the envelope an image flashed momentarily through his brain: he, a surgeon, running a scalpel diagonally across the chest of Steven Sinclair, opening an old wound.

He tried to sound businesslike, unemotional. "Certain . . . marks found on the Cooke girl's body. Indentations on the breasts and face, smaller but similar to the kind made by a branding iron."

Micah paused, but Sinclair said nothing, so he continued.

"The marks were identical to some found on one of D'Arbanville's victims in London. A Miss Amanda Wilding."

At the mention of the name, a pall, unlike anything Micah had ever experienced, fell over the room. It was as if Sinclair had evaporated and in his place was a shroud, covering all.

Micah, uncertain what to do next, laid out the photographs and autopsy reports on Tina Cooke and Amanda Wilding and left the room.

Sinclair didn't notice. He was in London. It was October 1980.

*   *   *

A fairly routine assignment: burgeoning new crime syndicate, headed by ersatz nobleman Lord Richard D'Arbanville, sweeping through the city. Indiscriminately eliminating operators, customers, and occasional bystanders. Bloodshed, havoc, and fear rampant. Confirm identities of leaders; locate and liquidate. Hope to get D'Arbanville before he smells trouble and runs.

Sinclair's contact in London was Oliver Wilding— ex-jockey, semiretired bookie, full-time tippler.

Oliver's penchant for figures and minutiae had naturally led him to keep detailed records of the recent turnover in the industry. He even had a map which showed a definite pattern to D'Arbanville's usurpation.

In exchange for protection and a small pension, Oliver agreed to turn over his records to the Fail-Safe Force and introduce Sinclair around as his apprentice and successor. The rest of the F.S. Force, Anderson and Kraddock and Mitchell, were infiltrating head-on as representatives of a Belgian syndicate seeking a merger with D'Arbanville's British operation.

As prearranged, on October 8 at 7:30, Sinclair rang the bell to Oliver Wilding's third-floor flat on Hempstead Row. The door was opened not by Wilding but by the most beautiful girl Sinclair had ever seen.

"Yes?" Almond-shaped green eyes stared at him inquiringly.

"I have an appointment with Mr. Wilding. My name is—"

"Sinclair." She accented the first syllable. "Father told me you were coming. He had to step out for a bit on business. Would you care to wait?" She motioned him into the room. Her voice was throaty and seductive, like honey over graham crackers.

Sinclair sat in an overstuffed blue chair, with yellowed doilies on the arms and back.

"I'm Amanda. Could I get you something to drink, Mr. Sinclair?"

"No. Thank you." He couldn't take his eyes off her, she was so lovely. She wore a white V-neck sweater and no bra. What he could glimpse of her breasts was magnificent. Almost as magnificent was the cascade of amber hair which framed her face. "Call me Steve."

She walked over to where he was seated and, bending from the waist, put her hands on the arms of his chair and lowered her head so that her eyes were level with his. "You're making me extremely nervous, Steven."

They both laughed; the sexual tension of a second ago melted away.

"So, Miss Amanda Wilding, who are you?"

When Oliver Wilding stumbled into his flat four hours and eleven pints later, he found that his daughter and his new apprentice had become very well acquainted.

Amanda was a secretary-turned-model-turned-dancer - turned - student - turned - waitress - turned-artist-turned-inward. She liked to say that Sinclair had caught her on the rebound from herself.

They made love every night for three weeks. After dinner at the flat, Sinclair and Oliver would go over the itinerary for the following day. Without fail at precisely 9:30, Oliver would lean back in his chair, put his hands on his stomach, and let out a deep sigh.

"Guess it's time for me to be slippin' off to the pub." He'd tug on the bill of his green cap, wink at his daughter, who pretended to be reading the newspaper, and strut, bowlegged, out the door. "Don't forget to leave a light on for me."

Amanda was as sexually abandoned as she was breathtakingly beautiful. "That's because I'm Pisces with Scorpio rising, and moon in Leo. You, I expect, are Capricorn with moon in Virgo, and"—she ran her index finger down along the timberline of black hairs that began at his chest—"Aries rising."

He kissed her breasts lightly, gently teasing the nipples. "Capricorn, yes. Moon, who cares? Rising . . . see for yourself."

They had discussed plans for the future, usually in the middle of the night between lovemaking.

Amanda wanted to continue her painting. "I suppose I could do that anywhere. But I'd like a studio. Someplace whose atmosphere was all me." She shook out her hair and, resting her chin on her fist, puckered her lips in what Sinclair had come to know as her "thoughtful" face. "With a skylight, and a bed in case I get all caught up in a canvas and don't want to leave . . ."

"Or want to entertain."

"Or want to entertain." She poked him playfully in the stomach. "And in one corner, mirrors and a barre, so that I may execute my jetés, pliés, and relevés, and fantasize about being a prima ballerina."

"Idyllic. Why did you give up dancing?"

She puckered again. "I was never really the right type. Physically, I mean. My bosom is too big."

"For some things, maybe."

"For the ballet, definitely. My dancing master used to warn me at least twice a day to wear a sturdy brassiere. 'Wouldn't want to give yourself a black eye, Amanda, luv.' I think he was joking."

"I think he was lusting."

"Actually, darling, I'm sure he was envying, if you receive my meaning."

"Check."

They watched the waning moon in silence for a moment.

He took her face in his hands, twining her soft hair between his fingers. "Have you ever been to America?"

"No. Why do you ask, as if I didn't know?"

"There's a house. In New Hampshire. Near the ocean." He looked into her luminous green eyes and saw clearly what he described. "With a stable, and an herb garden, and a maple tree. And the top floor of the three-story house—"

"Is my studio."

"Could be." He kissed her passionately.

"Darling, I don't know what to say."

"Yes."

"Of course yes. But what about father?"

"He'll come with us. He loves horses, you, and his bottle."

"Though not necessarily in that order."

"And he can have all three there. Besides, once this is over, he'll be much safer out of England."

"In that case, yes, yes, yes. I thought you'd never ask. It sounds too good to be true."

It was.

About a week later, they were lying in bed together when the phone rang.

Sinclair opened his eyes slowly, groggily checked his watch: 2:17. "Who could that be at this hour?"

"Probably father. Too bloody pissed to find his way home." She rolled over to answer it. "Hello." Listening, she suddenly sat up; a worried expression crossed her face. "Yes, yes he is. It's for you."

His eyes never left hers as he took the receiver and spoke. "This is Sinclair."

The voice on the other end of the line was high and singsongy. "Lord Richard D'Arbanville requests the pleasure of your company at number twenty-three Wiltby Place in one hour. If you value the life of Mr. Oliver Wilding, be there." The line went dead.

"Darling, what is it?"

"I don't know." He quickly dialed the Soames Hotel, where the rest of the F.S. Force was staying. "Room thirteen-nineteen please."

It was Kraddock who answered.

"Milt? This is Sinclair."

"Ah, Steve. I was just about to call you. We're going in."

"When?"

"Now. This morning. D'Arbanville's called a meeting of all his district representatives. He wants us to take a few thugs back to Belgium to seal our deal." Milt laughed his high cackle. "We can nail the whole operation."

"Why didn't you tell me about this?"

"I'm telling you about it now. Just happened

tonight. Anderson wants you to hang back with the explosives."

"Doesn't smell right to me."

"Might not be. That's why you're staying back to cover us. Is something wrong, Steve?"

Sinclair looked over at Amanda. "No, Milt. Everything's fine. Where and when?"

"The warehouse, like we figured."

"Right." He waited till Kraddock rang off and handed the receiver to Amanda.

"Father's in trouble, isn't he?"

"Why do you say that?"

"The way you looked at me just now. Please don't lie to me, Steven."

"I don't know. Maybe." He rolled out of bed. "That's what I have to go find out."

While he dressed neither of them said a word.

As Sinclair slipped on his jacket Amanda whispered, "Please hurry back. And be careful."

He nodded, his back to her, and left.

On his way to the Wiltby Place address, he stopped at his hotel room and picked up the explosives and his favorite .38. He loaded the former into the trunk of his Audi, the latter in his shoulder holster.

He arrived at 23 Wiltby Place five minutes ahead of schedule but way behind a demolition crew. It was a fenced yard of rubble. Not a person or car in sight, but taped to the gate of the chain-link fence was a note, written in pencil. It said: "Shell game—D'Arbanville 3; Sinclair 0. Where is Amanda?"

He drove as fast as he could to the Wilding flat. The front door was ajar. He found Oliver face-down on his bed, a note pinned to his back: "D'Arbanville 4, Sinclair 0. Time is running out."

What happened next Sinclair could not remember clearly. His mind had blocked out the pain. All that remained was a series of disconnected images.

He remembered driving in a blind fury; finding the bodies: of Anderson then Kraddock then Mitchell, a trail of breadcrumbs leading him to the warehouse; unloading his entire arsenal on D'Arbanville and his thugs; pulling the lifeless Amanda from the burning building.

*   *   *

He looked down at the pictures of Amanda on the table in front of him. If D'Arbanville were still alive . . .

"Ma, did that kid leave a number where he could be reached?"

"I told him to wait for you. His car's the red job parked round the back."

"Never could fool you, could I?"

Ma watched Sinclair walk out of the diner into the sunlight. Under his breath he said, "Mother knows best."

chapter 4

The car was a convertible, customized. The color, what Madison Avenue calls fire-engine red. White sidewall tires. Gleaming chrome. Gray fur upholstery.

Micah sat in the driver's seat, head tilted back to catch the early-afternoon rays. Mirrored sunglasses protected, hid the piercing black eyes.

Sinclair approached the convertible warily. He sensed the Librarian's fine hand in all this. The arrogant kid baiting, challenging him to prove his mettle. The dramatic trump card held back, revealed at the right moment to shock and shake him out of his apathy. Still, if it was D'Arbanville . . .

Sinclair tapped twice on the windshield. "No fuzzy dice?"

Micah didn't move a muscle. "Stolen in Vegas by a Jehovah's Witness."

Sinclair deftly lifted the sunglasses off the Cajun's face. "Take me to your leader." He flicked the sunglasses onto the dashboard.

"Sure thing, old man." The eyes popped open. Micah sat up, blinked a few times, and unlocked the passenger door.

Sinclair looked back toward the diner, nodded a few times slowly. Sighing, he pressed the button on the front door back into place, then jerked up the button on the rear door. He settled into the backseat, crooked elbow on silver-studded armrest.

"Drive."

Micah responded instantly.The car lurched forward before Sinclair had a chance to close his door. Dust swirled as the Cajun sped around the parking lot as though maneuvering through an obstacle course, turning sharply left, then right, then circling. Sinclair managed to get the door closed just in time to avoid a huge blue dumpster near the edge of the highway.

"Can you do a wheelie, too?" he asked with mock amazement as Micah thrust the convertible out into traffic.

"Sorry. Guess I'm a little hotheaded." He said it not as an apology, but as a simple statement of fact.

"No kidding."

"But that's why," Micah continued immediately, as though he hadn't heard Sinclair, "we're gonna be a fucking fantastic team. I'm one of the best operatives in the Association." Another flat statement. No brag, just fact.

"But I'm"—he shrugged—"a little unseasoned. I react too quickly, if that's possible. And the Librarian's right. I need a partner to take the edge off me, so to speak." He glanced back at Sinclair. "A little bit.

"You're older, you know the territory. You can

advise me, let me do the more strenuous work. I'd defer to your experience."

He ended his pitch with an ingratiating smile. Sinclair wondered how the Boy-Wonder grin would look with a few well-placed holes in it.

"You all through?" he asked quietly.

The question seemed to throw Micah off guard. He laughed unsteadily, the smile showing traces of tension.

"Because," Sinclair began with quiet authority, "if you don't shut up, I'm going to take your fucking head off, Junior."

The last hint of a grin left Micah's face, replaced by a look of surly indignation.

"Now listen real good, 'cause I'm sure the Librarian's gonna have a little quiz later. Ready? Okay. I am now a private citizen with no interest at all in the welfare of the quote free world unquote. And"—his voice suddenly rose in pitch and intensity—"I consider it an obscenity"—he raised high a tightly clenched fist—"to use a man's most painful, wrenching"—the fist dissolved slowly onto the car seat as he struggled for self-control. "I'm tired. I want to be left alone. And I'm sick to death of you spy-school graduates who think the whole thing is just a game, that nobody gets killed except the bad guys."

Neither man spoke for the rest of the drive.

Micah eased the convertible into a parallel parking space near the entrance to the library. Sinclair was out of the car before he had a chance to cut the engine.

"Come back for me in an hour."

"Wait a minute. What do you think I am? A chauffeur?"

Sinclair leaned over and pointed an index finger directly into Micah's face. "Never give a guy who hates your guts a straight line like that."

His face grim, he turned abruptly and began to jog up the long flight of steps that led to the revolving door.

Micah opened his mouth to shout an angry reply at the retreating figure, but decided against it. "Enough of the cocky-brat routine," he said to himself quietly. "Don't want to overdo it. The poor guy might take a genuine dislike to me."

He looked up at the sky. The sun still blazed against a cool blue background. "At least I got the old bull here." He let his body relax into the plush gray upholstery and closed his eyes.

"Sinclair!"

"You were expecting maybe Sean Connery? Long time, Pamela."

"Didn't Micah come with you?"

"I left the boy out at the hitching post with the horses."

Pamela frowned.

"Figured this showdown scene was written for two."

"I know the Librarian will want to see you right away."

"I know that, too. And I know that you know that I do. And I'm fairly confident that the Librarian knows that both of us know. We are, all in all, a fairly knowledgeable group. Now can we cut all this shit?"

She met his determined stare, unflinching. "Certainly, Sinclair. Follow me."

* * *

The study was dimly lighted. The Librarian sat motionless in his chair, whether in idleness or deep thought it was impossible to tell. Both hands rested lightly on the highly polished oak table. Dossiers sat, unevenly stacked, near the left hand, a hefty ceramic coffee mug near the right.

The two visitors entered the study silently, mesmerized, drawn into the hushed, almost reverent atmosphere of the room.

Pamela removed her glasses and squinted in the semidarkness. "Sinclair is here, sir. Alone. Is that all right?"

"Certainly." A rumbling monotone. "What happened to Micah?"

"He's—"

"You may return to your desk now, Pamela."

"But, sir—"

"That, I'm afraid, is an order, Pamela."

"Yes, sir."

"You may draw the shades and lock up the building. Mr. Sinclair will be my last appointment."

"Yes, sir."

"If the general calls, put him through. Otherwise, I'm gone for the day."

"Yes, sir." She put on her best officiously brisk manner and walked stiffly toward the door.

"Oh, and Pamela."

"Yes, sir?"

"You needn't be so disappointed. You know I always discuss all my meetings with you. We'll have a nice long talk about Mr. Sinclair this evening, right after MacNeil-Lehrer."

Pamela was too shocked and embarrassed to reply. She scurried out of the study as fast as her shapely legs would carry her.

The Librarian was nonchalant. "Pamela fancies herself an enigma. A female Clark Kent, if you will. She doesn't like to be"—he lifted his coffee mug and took a sip—"exposed."

"Who does?"

"Touché, Steve."

"I didn't come here to trade quips with you."

"I know that."

"I want you to leave me alone."

"You know I can't do that, Steve."

"I do?"

"Yes. Otherwise you wouldn't be here."

"I'm here to plead, demand, do whatever's necessary to get you and your band of juvenile-delinquent agents off my case, permanently. I did more than my share. God and country have taken as much of my hide as they're entitled to."

"It's not that simple. It—"

"Never is, I know."

"I was going to say, it isn't a question of 'shares,' or obligations; it's a question of need. The needs of the Association, of the free world . . ."

"The free world!? Christ."

"Yes. You find the expression ridiculous?"

"In a word, highly."

"You didn't used to."

"People change."

"Exactly. I was talking about your needs too, Steve."

Sinclair had no answer for this. It wasn't what he expected.

The Librarian took another swallow of coffee and continued. "First, let me apologize for the devious way in which I brought you here today. You gave me no alternative."

"You could have respected my wishes and left me alone."

"Where would that have gotten us, Steve?"

"The end justifies the means?"

"Usually."

"Convenient philosophy, for the side with the means. Might makes right."

"I thought we weren't going to trade quips."

"Check. Say what you have to say."

The Librarian paused meaningfully before leaning back in his chair to speak. "Our meeting today was as necessary as it was inevitable. Whether you believe me or not, I take full responsibility for what happened in London. We seriously underestimated D'Arbanville's vindictiveness, and the consequences were tragic."

"Luckily, you're still alive."

"So are you, Steve, whether you want to face it or not."

Bastard, Sinclair thought. "Go on."

"I don't mean to diminish your personal grief, but the fact is, these disasters occur from time to time. Bluntly, it's in the line of duty."

"Stiff upper lip?"

"If you like. The old Fail-Safe Force was staggeringly successful. Not a casualty in thirty-eight missions. Their destruction was simply the result of a carelessness born of overconfidence. There's nothing you personally could have done."

"I let D'Arbanville lead me around by the nose, like a fucking amateur."

"You're very hard on yourself."

"Just realistic."

"No." The Librarian leaned forward toward Sinclair, daring him to disagree. "That is why you are here today. A realist faces facts. In your position he either stays with the Association or comes in—after accepting the fact that the past cannot be changed. A painfully simple choice.

"The Association brings operatives in periodically as a matter of course. We issue new identities, give fresh starts. You know that as well as I do. That greasy spoon you habituate is virtually the Association's V.F.W. hall.

"That option was, and is, open to you. But you have chosen instead to hide and lick your wounds. . . ."

Sinclair opened his mouth to protest, but the Librarian cut him off quickly. "Or whatever you call it. Let me finish. Please, Steve. I know that you needed time. Taking into account your unblemished record, I tried to give it to you.

"It simply didn't work. You're still bitter, lethargic. You're no closer to accepting the tragedy than you were three years ago when it happened." He clasped his hands together tightly in a gesture that was half pleading, half prodding. "It's time to come in or come back, Steve."

"You're right," Sinclair said simply. "But"—he shook his head wistfully—"I can't come up with one good reason to do either."

"Need." The Librarian tossed the top dossier from the stack across the table.

"Back to that again." The file landed at the table's edge, directly in front of him. D'Arbanville's face smirked up at Sinclair from the cover. "You're sure about this?"

"Absolutely. Same physical description. Same M.O. Same calling card—I take it you saw the photographs?"

Sinclair nodded.

"I'm assembling a team to go to Bangkok and infiltrate D'Arbanville's operation. Micah will head up our Thai mission." He hefted a very thick file.

"Micah?" Sinclair laughed. "That smart-ass punk you sent to piss me off?"

The Librarian chose to ignore Sinclair's remark. "Our most successful young operative. He's unseasoned, but remarkably skillful."

"Skip the testimonial. He sang his own praises on the way over here."

"That's characteristic. Micah's very rough around the edges, but he's undeniably effective. His record speaks for itself."

Sinclair couldn't decide whether this, too, was one of the Librarian's little ploys. Was he suddenly supposed to volunteer to take over, go to Thailand, sacrifice his carcass for Mom and apple pie? Bull*shit*, he thought. "You're the boss," he said almost under his breath. "What do you want me to do?"

"Basically, as much or as little as you like. This is definitely not a solo mission. Micah needs a partner to accompany him overseas."

"Forget it. I'm not playing Gabby Hayes to his John Wayne."

"Of course. Given your mutual antagonism, I would never suggest such a thing. You can always change your mind if you find you are able to come to some working understanding with Micah.

"I am trying to build a new group of agents that will fill the void created when the Fail-Safe Force was destroyed. It will be difficult, I know. It may be impossible. But I have to try.

"My reasons for offering you this mission are

twofold. I hope that you will use it as an opportunity to exact the vengeance you deserve on D'Arbanville. You can't, of course, recoup your losses, but perhaps you can burn away some of the grief which is gnawing you by obtaining your pound of flesh.

"Also, you may discover that working for the Association again will put direction, meaning of some sort, back into your life."

Part of Sinclair wanted to laugh, but he saw that the Librarian was deadly serious. His mind resisted, stubbornly, and he wondered.

The Librarian continued. "I want you to work on the preliminary investigative work, here in the States. Then, if you think you're ready, I can easily integrate you with the team that's going to Thailand."

"Headed by Micah."

"If you decide to go"—the Librarian allowed a flicker of a smile to appear on his face—"headed by you."

"Uh-huh. Finally, the other shoe drops." Sinclair smiled, too, in spite of himself. "You really are the Master Bastard, aren't you?"

The Librarian proceeded, straight-faced. "My official title is Master Bastard, Esquire. Whether or not you stay with the Association, I want you on this mission, Steve. Your knowledge of D'Arbanville and his M.O. is invaluable."

"Your second reason?"

"I'd like you to oversee the selection of the new F.S. Force. Evaluate all potential candidates."

"Meaning little Mr. Micah?"

"Micah is head and shoulders above any and all operatives of comparable age."

"He's a royal pain in the ass. That's my official evaluation. Sir."

"His record closely parallels your own at twenty-five."

"No hitting below the belt."

"Noted. Micah's skills are extraordinary in terms of depth as well as diversity. He's used to working alone and needs to make some . . . adjustments. I'm sure that after you read his file"—he hefted it again—"you'll understand Micah a lot better." He slid the bulky cloth folder across the table, where it lay untouched.

"Sir," Sinclair began again, trying to sound reasonable, "the first, the major, the only prerequisite for team fieldwork is the ability to cooperate and follow orders. This"—*be tactful*, a voice inside him shouted—"young man, no matter how skilled, is a maverick. He'll never work smoothly with other operatives."

"That remains to be seen. At this point, the rewards far outweigh the risks. If you'll read his file, and work with him stateside, I guarantee you that I will accept your evaluation as the last word."

"Fine." Sinclair took hold of Micah's dossier and placed it on top of the D'Arbanville file in front of him.

The Librarian stood up to indicate that the meeting had come to an end. "Thank you, Steve. Good to have you aboard again." He extended his right hand.

Sinclair shook it professionally. "We'll see," he said flatly.

He'd been had, and he knew it.

chapter 5

The red convertible cut in and out of the high-speed superhighway traffic as if it had a mind of its own. Micah was more than competent at the wheel, Sinclair admitted reluctantly. Still, he had wanted to take charge of the driving himself.

Instinct, maybe. Maybe to show Boy Wonder who was boss. Maybe to show himself who was. Maybe, an inner voice spoke firmly, you should can the pointless meditation and go with the flow for a while. That's how you got into this ass-backwards mess in the first place.

He contented himself with the file resting on his lap; not the D'Arbanville file—that he knew practically by heart; not the dossier all about the mysterious Micah no-name—that he was saving for later. This was a file containing as much information as The Association could find on one Jezebel Cooke. (Except why her parents had elected to call her Jezebel).

After his meeting with the Librarian, Sinclair had been quickly ushered outside by a tight-lipped

Pamela. When he reached the top of the library steps, the red convertible was nowhere in sight.

He checked his watch. Well over an hour. Micah had probably sneaked off to smoke a joint and nurse his bruised ego.

A rough tap on the shoulder forced Sinclair out of his speculation. He steeled himself for a possible fight and spun briskly around. There was Micah, sporting a gold-braided chauffeur's uniform and monogrammed cap. He swung the cap in a wide arc to his underarm and bowed low. "The car is here . . . sir," he uttered with a vaguely New England accent.

Sinclair hoped somebody was keeping score.

Micah slowly raised himself to a standing position and handed Sinclair a dossier, extending his right arm slowly up and out like a ballet dancer's. (The file concerned Jezebel Cooke.) He pivoted neatly and led Sinclair to the waiting convertible.

Micah flipped on the radio and "Born to Be Wild" invaded the interior of the car. He hummed along atonally. Sinclair derived a certain satisfaction from the knowledge that Micah could not carry a tune in a bucket.

He opened the file.

Jezebel Cooke, twenty-eight years old, was the elder of Marilyn and Senator Toby Cooke's two daughters, now Marilyn and Toby's only daughter. Her early life was represented sketchily: a xeroxed birth certificate, courtesy of Houston General; school records; a blurred snapshot of two little red-haired girls playing on a backyard jungle gym. He held on to the photograph as he paged through the file.

Toby Cooke was a senator and a Texan. He spoiled his children as any man of his wealth and stature would. Yet, despite private tutors and parental bribery, Jezebel still managed to screw up in any school the Cooke money could weasel her into. She graduated high school next to last in her class. She also had the fourth highest score in the statewide college board exams.

While Tina plodded along determinedly, earning a solid B minus average, Jezebel had gone on to a variety of classes. She spoke fluent Russian, she could cook dim sum, she just couldn't seem to stay put for very long.

When the senator retired, he accepted a post in public relations for a computer firm based in Kyoto. Should have studied Japanese, Jezebel, Sinclair thought wryly. Mom and Dad elected to stay in Japan while Tina and Jezebel returned to the States. There, Tina pursued an acting career, garnering along the way a failed marriage and a few small roles in some kung-fu films. Jezebel worked at a variety of jobs; some interesting, some boring, some downright ludicrous.

Currently, she was a martial-arts instructor at a swank midtown health spa. Steve grinned, imagining the plump matrons opting for a quick lesson in karate before the sauna or after the hot tub. When she wasn't teaching, she was being taught, honing her skills for some yet, unknown battle. Maybe that moment was at hand.

He closed the file, giving his full attention to the photograph.

Even without the difference in ages, which was slight, he would have known one sister from the other. Tina had the slightly spoiled air of a girl

who knows just how pretty she is and just how far
it'll take her. She leaned against the painted leg of
the backyard gym coyly.

Jezebel seemed more serious, more square of
jaw, and somehow, even as a child, more womanly.
Her eyes looked beyond the photographer, fastened
on some unseen object of interest.

He slipped the photo back into the file and held
it out to Micah. Micah was still bopping along
with Steppenwolf. Sinclair tapped him on the shoulder with the file; he waved it away.

"I've read it. So . . ." He downshifted smoothly.
"What do you think of the surviving Miss Cooke?"

"I'll wait till I meet the lady in person. Still . . ."

"Say it," Micah prompted.

"I keep wondering what it is she's looking for.
That make any sense?" Sinclair was pretty sure it
didn't, not to the Cajun. Emotional depth was not
his specialty.

Micah flipped off the radio. "Sure it does."

He spoke so quietly Sinclair had to replay the
words in his head to make sure that was what he'd
really said.

Beautiful Universe Spa was not exactly what they
were expecting. In addition to the pedicures,
manicures, and swimming pools, Beautiful Universe provided more than adequate instruction and
equipment for a student of the martial arts.

After the young aide had given up trying to sell
them lifetime memberships, they'd been taken to
"Miss Cooke's eleven-thirty self-defense."

It was S.R.O., the red wrestling mat ringed three
deep by tunic-clad students. The class was predomi-
nantly male.

Sinclair and Micah settled inconspicuously at the outer fringe of the group, quietly observing the lady in charge.

Jezebel Cooke wore the sunflower-yellow tunic and loose trousers that was de rigueur for all Beautiful Universe staff members, but even that outfit could not disguise her well-formed and well-trained body.

She pivoted on bare feet, explaining a few simple moves to the class. As she spoke in a soft well-modulated voice—(Sinclair remembered, she'd been a tour guide at the UN for a while)—she demonstrated the moves, her hands gracefully shaping air, then suddenly slashing through it, sleeves fluttering with a soft "whuh" sound.

"You're the martial artist," Sinclair said to Micah. "How's her form."

"Her form's great," Micah answered. "But I've never seen a style quite like that."

A hand timidly went up among the students, and a young woman, fiddling with the white belt of her ghee, asked a question. "How does a woman, no matter how skilled, measure up against a man?"

"Always one of my favorite questions," Micah whispered.

Jezebel seemed suitably pissed off and chose the biggest bruiser in the group she could find.

He ambled onto the mats, grinning shyly. There was a glint in his eye.

Jezebel took her stance, balanced and easy.

He rushed, lashing out in a whirling kick aimed for her throat. It whistled past harmlessly as she jerked her head backward. Before he could recover his balance, she dove in, planting one foot squarely on the foot he was standing on. He was immobilized, and left looking pretty foolish.

She shoved him lightly and he toppled over helplessly.

Jezebel turned back to her class. "Does that answer your question?"

Behind her the bruiser leaped, only to crash-land after another patented Jez Cooke sidestep. He kicked and chopped viciously, never connecting once.

"He'll rip her apart, if he ever gets to land a punch." Micah commented.

"She won't let him."

Sinclair was right. Jezebel continued to dance in a manner even Fred Astaire would have been proud of. Her opponent was less impressed; he'd gotten the bit in his teeth and was determined to knock teacher flat on her shapely ass, despite her cues that the demonstration had come to an end. After a hurried peek at her watch, Jez faked a high kick, switched legs in midair, and struck behind the bruiser's knees. He went down and she got him in a choke-hold, letting him up only after his face had gone a deep purple.

Sinclair laughed deeply. "The Dr. Tanaka sleeper hold! That's why you can't peg her style!"

"Dr. Tanaka?"

"Sure, little Japanese guy, around a thousand years old, used to coach on the professional wrestling circuit. I don't know where she dug him up"—he shook his head admiringly—"but that's where she learned her stuff."

"Well, you can ask her in person."

Jezebel was cutting through the crowd, making

her way toward them deliberately. She did not look happy.

Sinclair reached into his pocket for his ID. That little piece of plastic had an almost mystic ability to calm people down.

Not Jezebel Cooke. "Don't bother," she said in that smooth voice. "I know who you are and why you're here. Just give me a minute to change and we can discuss what took you so long."

The two men watched her retreating.

"Too bad Dr. Tanaka wasn't running a charm school," Micah commented.

chapter 6

A half hour later, they were sitting at the spa's juice bar. Jezebel had changed into a turquoise jumpsuit, the belt knotted at her supple waist.

Sinclair was doing his best to ignore the glass of carrot juice in front of him, although Jezebel and Micah seemed to have no problem with it.

"She must have told you something about the job with Dreamscape Films," Micah was saying.

"Not really. Tina knew I really didn't understand too much about show business. She said it was a good part but a lot of hard work. Some people in the crew didn't think a woman belonged in an action film, mixing it up with the guys."

"What people?"

Jezebel shrugged. "No one in particular. Tina wasn't one to complain."

"Miss Cooke." Sinclair tried to be as diplomatic as he could. "Thailand is notorious for its drug traffic. Could your sister have—"

"No!" she exploded. "She never even took an aspirin."

"No one likes to think of a close relative as an addict—"

"Not Tina." She was emphatic. "Not drugs, not alcohol, not men. After she and Don broke up—he was an actor, too—there was nobody. Tina said her career came first." She dug into her large handbag. "I kept most of her letters. Maybe you can find something I overlooked."

"Thank you." Sinclair accepted the packet of letters she held out to him and started reading one at random. "Who are Godzilla and Mothra?"

Micah perked up. "Japanese monsters."

"Cats," Jezebel explained, "Two sealpoint Siamese Tina sent to me from Thailand."

"I'd like to hold on to these for a while." At her nod, he slipped the letters into his attaché case. He scribbled the number of Ma's Diner on his card and handed it to her. "If you remember anything, call this number. Ask for Ma, then leave your message."

She pocketed the card. "May I ask you a question, now?"

Sinclair nodded.

"What the hell are you two assholes still doing in this country?"

Micah's jaw was hanging open; Sinclair was pretty sure he was sporting the same expression.

"Why aren't you in Thailand catching those bastards?" she went on. "Do you know the kind of red tape I'm going through just to bury my sister in the States? Not to mention the valuable time I'm wasting fielding questions and innuendos from you two." Anger diffused northern lights into her cool blue eyes. "I am a tax-paying citizen, and if you boys don't get on the stick, I'm going to see to it that you take a cut in pay!"

With the same quick movements she'd used in the gym, she left, her body seething with silky rage.

Jezebel Cooke had found her mission.

Lieutenant Juan Valjenos paced the floor of his oak-paneled office with short measured steps. The sound of his boot heels regularly meeting the wood underfoot played a staccato accompaniment to the lecture he was delivering. He walked in a perfect square, around and around a small bespectacled man who was seated in a chair in the middle of the room.

"So you see, Gogee, you have acted very, very, irresponsibly. By holding on to the film, and the merchandise, you have caused a serious delay in our traffic flow, a delay which will ultimately cost us several thousands of dollars, undoubtedly damage our reputation internationally, and possibly encourage others to follow your example. The consequences could be disastrous. And yet, you come here today, demand to see me, and ask, not for forgiveness, but for more money. I am frankly appalled, and, oh, so disappointed in you."

Valjenos paused to allow the full effect of his words to sink in and then continued his relentless march around the little man. "I am sure you realize the gravity of the situation. What have you to say?"

Gogee raised his head to face his boss, but Valjenos continued his pacing, eyes focused on an imaginery point a foot in front of him. So Gogee

stared down at the floor between his feet and tried
to make his voice sound deep and strong and sure.

"I been with the organization since the beginning.
Gave up my own profitable racket to join up. Always deliver faithful service. But I never get no
place. No raise. No promotion. Cost of livin' keeps
goin' up. I want more. Never mind your fuckin'
fancy talk. You know I deserve it. Just cut me in. I
got your film. And the goods. If you want 'em,
deliver."

Gogee punctuated his final statement by stamp-
ing his foot in time to his words. I wish he'd stop
that fuckin' pounding, he thought to himself. Click-
click, click-click. He suddenly realized that he was
breathing so heavily he could hear it. His heartbeat was pulsing in his ears.

As if reading Gogee's mind, Valjenos abruptly
halted.

"I see," he said, and walked over to his desk. "Of
course, you leave me no alternative." He pushed a
button near the telephone.

Almost immediately, two burly men in dark
suits appeared and stood expectantly in the office
doorway.

Valjenos nodded and turned toward his large
bay window, which overlooked downtown Bangkok.

The two men quickly attacked the helpless Gogee.
One held him by the throat while the other tied
him securely to the chair.

When he was firmly bound and flanked by the
two thugs, Valjenos spun around to face him. "I
hope you realize that this is nothing personal,
Gogee. In fact, I even like you. You've been very
loyal, and valuable, to the organization. Until now.
But you must understand my position. Your imper-

tinence cannot go unpunished." He nodded at his two henchmen and again turned his back.

One of the two men pulled a silver cigarette lighter from his trouser pocket. Gogee watched with frightened eyes as the other grabbed a handful of Gogee's yellow cotton shirt, near the belt, and pulled up. His huge fist slammed into Gogee's jaw, dazing him momentarily. Then, slowly and delicately, the thug lifted the shirttail until it was on a level with Gogee's eyes. The one with the lighter flicked until he had a tall flame and ignited the shirt. The other one dropped it into Gogee's lap.

Valjenos suddenly spoke, his back still turned. "It will burn very slowly. Now. You will tell me what I want to know. Where have you hidden my merchandise?"

Gogee could barely feel the burning in his lap, but the numbing aftereffect of the blow, the pressure of the ropes holding him to the chair, the presence of the thugs hovering over him, the steady drone of Valjenos's voice, and his own racing thoughts about how to escape combined to stun him into silence.

Valjenos continued smoothly. "Realize. That it is only a matter of time. That you will tell me eventually. Why wait until the pain becomes unbearable?"

Gogee suddenly remembered seeing a movie in which a spy who was being tortured made himself pass out by breathing real hard and fast. When the spy came to, he was in a big open field with a lot of dead soldiers. He'd waited till dark and got away. Maybe Gogee could do that, too.

Valjenos was still talking. "There is no possibility of escape. Talk, and we may come to some understanding. Are you listening to me?"

Gogee didn't answer. Valjenos spun around, intending to roar his captive into submission, and saw immediately what Gogee was up to. The little fool was panting inaudibly, mouth open. His eyes were tightly closed, as if in prayer.

Valjenos's mouth twisted into a half smile. He signaled to his men. The one with the lighter flicked and brought the flame under Gogee's ear.

Gogee screamed in shock and pain, but the flame stayed where it was, burning.

Valjenos's voice remained calm but increased in volume to cover Gogee's howls of anguish. "Where is it?"

"I don't know! I don't know!" He could smell the tender flesh of his earlobe roasting and feel the slowly creeping fire in his midsection as it scorched his belly. "Oh, God, stop it! Please stop!"

"It's very simple, Gogee. Tell, and it stops."

"Awright, awright! It's in the trunk of my car."

"Parked downstairs?"

"No. At the theater." The pain was so unbearable that he started to cry.

"Ling." Valjenos signaled to the one with the lighter. Ling released his thumb and the tiny flame died. Valjenos opened a drawer in his desk, pulled out a large red towel, and tossed it to his other gorilla, Chee, who quickly smothered the burning shirt. Gogee's head flopped onto his chest like a puppet's.

Valjenos walked crisply over to the chair and planted his feet squarely in front of the semiconscious man. Ling grabbed a hank of hair near Gogee's forehead and yanked up. The little man gasped involuntarily. He still breathed, but his eyes were glassy, pointed at the ceiling.

Valjenos spat in disgust. "Pah! No character." Ling loosened his grip, and the head fell again to its resting position. "Chee. Retrieve the merchandise. Break the lock. Our friend is in no condition to tell us where to find the keys."

Chee strode out of the office.

Valjenos pulled a slender greenish-brown cigar from his inside jacket pocket. The cellophane wrapping crackled as he removed it. He rolled the fragrant cigar between his hands, savoring the aroma. "The second best sensual experience known to man." He smiled dreamily.

He strolled to the door, while Ling wrapped the large red towel tightly around Gogee's head. Valjenos stopped abruptly in the doorway. "Ling?"

"Yes, sir?"

"May I borrow your lighter?"

"Of course, sir." Ling fumbled for a moment in his pocket and brought out both his lighter and a revolver. The former he tossed to his boss.

Valjenos closed the door softly behind him. As he took the first puff he heard the muffled gunshot. Perfect, he thought to himself.

Ling appeared a moment later. "Sir, should I dispose of the body now?"

"What? Uh, as you wish. Chee should be back shortly. You can wait for him to help you." Valjenos blew out a long jet of smoke. "I shall have to call Europe and inform Lord D. of our slight difficulty."

Halfway across the world, in an Amsterdam hotel suite, Richard D'Arbanville lolled on a blue satin bedspread, clad only in a towel. His left hand lay near an antique pewter tray on which rested a silver monogrammed spoon and traces of white powder. His right hand fondled the creamy white thighs of a twelve-year-old prostitute named Liesl.

Liesl fed him raw clams, from the half shell. Delicately seasoned, they slid easily over his palate and down. He savored each stage of the dollops' journey through his taste buds.

The ringing of the phone was a less than welcome interruption. D'Arbanville sat up slowly, opened his eyes, and snapped his fingers. Liesl handed him the phone and disappeared with the plate of food.

"Yes?"

"Lord D.?"

D'Arbanville didn't speak for a minute, but Valjenos could faintly hear him breathing over the line. Finally, he said in a flat voice, "Continue."

Valjenos cleared his throat before speaking. "I'm calling because there's been a small problem with one of our distributors. It's all been taken care of, but the shipment will be a couple of days late. Nothing to worry about." He coughed. "I just didn't want you to worry, or wonder about the delay."

"Thoughtful. What exactly was the problem?"

"Greed."

D'Arbanville's voice rose slightly, became more sharp and deliberate. "I did not ask for your piercing psychological insights, Lieutenant. I simply want to know what exactly happened."

"Yes, sir." Why did he always call him "lefttenant"? "One of the local distributors, a projectionist named Gogee Loo, tried to blackmail me. He hid the shipment and demanded to be made a partner."

"And?"

"I persuaded him to disclose the location and eliminated him."

"How?"

"In the usual manner."

D'Arbanville sighed. "You are far too impetuous, my dear boy. Mr. Loo was a loyal employee, with seniority and friends among the lower echelon."

Valjenos's tone became suddenly hostile. "Are you saying that you disapprove of my methods?"

"I'm merely saying that I would have handled the matter in a different manner."

"You have placed me in charge of the entire Far East operation."

"Quite." D'Arbanville paused to examine his exquisitely manicured nails. "The merchandise, then, is intact."

"Chee is picking it up now."

"You mean"—D'Arbanville gripped the satin bedspread as if it were Valjenos's neck he held—"you killed that man without knowing whether what he told you was true?"

"He was too stupid to lie. Besides, I was sick of the sight of his yellow face."

"I will be on the next plane to Bangkok. Replace Mr. Loo with a reliable local. I hope, for your sake, that you are correct in your assumptions." D'Arbanville hung up before Valjenos had a chance to reply.

Fucking blueblood prick, Valjenos thought.

D'Arbanville stared hard at the gold ring he wore on the smallest finger of his left hand. His most prized possession. The band was twisted, coiled to represent the body of a killer python. The ring's face was the snake's head, two perfect blue diamonds the eyes. When D'Arbanville was upset or confused, he looked into the depths of the python's eyes. It told him what to do.

chapter 7

It had not been a gold-star day, Jez thought, balancing a bag of groceries on one hip as she fished for her house keys. Funny how your mind could play leapfrog like that; gold stars made her think of grade school, which made her think of those perfectly awful vinyl pocketbooks they'd clamored for, she and Tina. . . .

She pushed through the door into the vestibule. Get the mail, she told herself stubbornly; get the mail and stop thinking about Tina. One hand reached into the mailbox; the little metal box jabbed at the soft flesh of her hand.

Lot of pain in this world, Jez old girl, she thought, mounting the stairs. Walk-ups lost their charm with relative speed. By the fifth floor, she could hear Mothra and Godzilla yowling the chow-chow-chow call.

"Hang on, guys!" she called out, stepping into the neat little apartment. Before she could set the mail down on the kitchen table, her feet and legs were assailed by wriggling feline bodies. Dinner was late, but they intended to forgive her, the hoarse meows announced.

Hurriedly, she poured the dry unappetizing cat chow into one large bowl. (Mothra and Godzilla were very cooperative.) It looked awful. At the last moment, she relented and added a little leftover chicken from last night's dinner.

In proper cat fashion, they snapped up the chicken and then stalked away, tails proudly waving, as if they'd done a wonderful thing, refusing to eat that garbage.

"You'll eat it when you get hungry enough. Gourmet cats," she scoffed. "Gourmet cats Tina had to send me. Thanks, Tina." *Tina* . . . she shook her head. I won't think about her now. But she knew she was going to, all the same.

After the hair-pulling and infantile teasing of childhood was over, Tina and Jezebel had gotten along like best friends. Together they conspired against their father's strictness, sneaking from the house, giggling, to meet some boys at the movies. Even then they both liked kung-fu movies. They would jump around the foyer, chopping and kicking and striving to outdo each other's imitations of Bruce Lee's distinctive yelps. Jez had accidentally pulverized her mother's prize vase; it was an heirloom to boot. She'd stood there while Tina took the blame.

Tina was Daddy's favorite and was sure she'd get off with a lighter sentence.

That hadn't mattered to Jez. It was Tina standing there, shouldering her petty crime that she remembered, would always remember.

It was Tina who convinced her to study the martial arts in Kyoto, but it was Jez who talked her younger sister into returning to the States to pursue her acting career.

"You can do it, Tina!" she'd urged. "If you want to be an actress, just make up your mind and do it!"

"I don't know, Jez." Tina had smiled wistfully. "I'm not smart like you."

Well, Jez had done a real fine thing, sending her own sister to a violent death.

She flicked on the TV, hoping some old movie would distract her, anything was better than the train of thought whistling through her brain.

". . . and on the local front . . . six teenagers robbed and stabbed an elderly news vendor. . . ."

She killed the evening news and started going through the mail. Ma Bell wanted her pound of flesh, and there was a notice from Beautiful Universe: they were raising their rates again. Jez couldn't believe what people were willing to pay just to sweat in a lavish setting.

The local supermarket was proud to announce a sale on ground chuck, provided Jez bought ten pounds of the stuff. There was a letter from Mother: "Long distance is so expensive, dear." And last in the pile was a letter from Tina.

A letter from the other side of the grave.

She dropped the flimsy air-mail envelope like a hot coal.

A letter from Tina Cooke, postmarked on the day she died.

Jez ripped at it with shaking fingers. The thin sheets slid out of the envelope past her fingers. After a few ineffectual sallies, she got a firm hold on the crinkly paper. She began to read.

Weak sobs escaped her. It was just another long,

chatty, Tina letter, damn the extra postage, full
speed ahead. What had she been expecting anyhow?
Some secret message only visible with Jez Cooke's
secret decoder ring? Yeah, you bet. Only in the
movies, girl, she told herself.

But she read it anyway.

Dear Jez,
Hiya, kiddo, how's life in the big city? Thailand
is lovely this time of year (more mosquitos per
square foot than you got hairs on your head)
and even us big stars are running out of Caladryl
lotion.

I really do wish you were here, this fight scene
I'm working on is so tough. I'm supposed to
take out this 200-pound elephant turd Sammy
Wuan (what a nasty shit!). Half the people here
are real creeps; this guy Juan Valjenos is the
top of my list. A creep and a lech. But he's
really tight with the producer, so you can bet
he'll be here long after little Tina has come and
gone. Ain't the movies fun?

Mothra and Godzilla, a little sadder and hungrier,
were going back to their dish. Jez rubbed her eyes
wearily. Tina's cramped hand was not easy to read.
She decided to skip down.

. . . and then he threw me . . .

Further down.

. . . but Tim Chang told him that . . .

And flipped to the second page. Get out your secret decoder, Jez, she told herself, for the second

page was written in a different pén and in a far more desperate hand.

They are going to kill me. They think I know something, and they are going to kill me. At least Sammy won't ... no more Sammy.... What do they think I know?''

There was a third sheet of paper with a single line on it.

From the ridiculous to the sublime ...

Jez read it over a dozen times and it still didn't make any sense, other than being a rather trite figure of speech. Why would Tina, minutes before her death, send Jez this cryptic message? Or had she meant to leave it for someone else?

Jez still couldn't make heads or tails of it. But she knew someone who could.

Godzilla had curled up on her handbag and she had to throw him off before she could get to the card Steve Sinclair had given her.

Lucille was polishing spoons.

Ma had this thing about spoons which was just beyond Lucille. They came out of the dishwasher clean enough; Lucille thought Ma's mania about spoons had to do with the appellation "greasy spoon." So here she was polishing the blankety-blank spoons.

The phone rang.

"Ruby!" she yelled.

"Keep your shirt on." Ruby grabbed the phone and listened for a second. Her braying laugh joined

Linda Ronstadt wailing her poor, poor, pitiful heart out on the juke.

"Oh, Mother!" Ruby laughed. "I got a lady on the line for you." He took the phone from her. "A lady who don't know you very well . . . Mother."

Ma could have cut her down fast, but he was a little excited. He'd been expecting this call.

"Hello, Mother?"

He winced. "Ma will do just fine, Miss Cooke."

"Oh." She didn't have to say anything for him to realize he'd made a mistake. He shouldn't have let on that he knew her name. The Librarian had been explicit; no way was Miss Cooke to be made aware that the Association was . . . interested in her.

Ma decided not to fly solo on this one. "Can you hold on, miss? I'd like to transfer you to my private line."

"Well, all right."

He hit a small button on the underside of the phone and hung up. "That's a wrong number, all right," he called out to Ruby and Lucille. "Lady thought we were some kind of fancy tea shop." They laughed. "I'm going to my office."

One of the buttons on the phone was flashing. Ma was real glad he hadn't scared off Miss Cooke. He just had a little housekeeping to do before he could get back to her.

He shoved the stack of newspapers off the card table: the uppermost one said NIXON RESIGNS (one of Ma's favorites). Hiding underneath was a computer keyboard. A similar terminal sat in the Librarian's study. From beneath an upended carton, Ma yanked a monitor which fit onto the keyboard neatly.

He flipped the power on.

From his study, the Librarian typed, PROCEED, MOTHER . . . onto the monitor.

Ma swore softly. He was never going to hear the end of that. "Miss Cooke? Still with me?"

"Sure, Ma."

He smiled. She had a lovely voice. Ma was a sucker for those pear-shaped tones.

"I was hoping, Ma, that you could tell me where to get in touch with Steve Sinclair?"

SINCLAIR UNAVAILABLE TILL A.M . . . the Librarian typed.

"Uh, I don't know where Steve's at tonight. Can I help you?"

She hesitated a long second.

DON'T PUSH . . . read the monitor.

Jez continued. "I have a letter from my sister, postmarked April sixth."

The Librarian typed, SISTER TINA, DECEASED 4/6 . . . 016. . . .

O-one-six was code for a violent murder under investigation.

"I'd like Mr. Sinclair to see it."

SINCLAIR STILL QT? . . . Ma typed slowly.

YES . . .

Ma sighed. "I wish I knew where he was, Miss Cooke."

SISTER . . . flashed on the screen.

"We're all very sorry about your sister."

"We?"

"Mr. Sinclair and me, we work for the same people. . . ."

"Yes, I know. Sort of an organization."

GO ON . . .

Ma cleared his throat. "The Association."

"So." Her voice was thoughtful. "It does exist. I thought Mr. Sinclair was FBI or CIA. . . ."

"No."

"Well, I guess Mr. Sinclair can pick the letter up."

NOW PUSH . . . the screen instructed.

"Could you bring it over here? I'll give you the address. Another gentleman in our group would like to talk to you."

She sighed. "I don't know."

"It was wrong for your sister to die like that, Miss Cooke," Ma said quietly. "I didn't know her, but even from her file, she seemed like a real sweet kid. Now she's gone, and with what the papers are printing about her, I don't know what your parents are going through." Over the phone he could hear her struggling with the inevitable tears. He really hated doing this.

PUSH . . .

The computer had no heart.

"We're doing all we can," Ma continued, "but we need your help. We need your help to catch those rats that killed Tina."

Her voice was scarcely audible. "Tell me what I have to do."

He gave her the address of the library. Pamela would be waiting for her. He hung up.

THANK YOU, MOTHER . . . the Librarian typed.

FUCK YOU, JACK . . . Ma typed.

The monitor went dark.

From a desk drawer, Ma pulled out an envelope. Inside was a passport, a Screen Actors Guild card, various waivers and work permits; all prepared for Jezebel Cooke. The Librarian sure was thorough.

Still, this whole scene had put a damper on his evening. He hoped Steve was having a better one.

chapter 8

He did not have the TV on. He did not have the radio on. Unlike most people, Sinclair did not mind the particular frequency of silence. Usually.

He had not yet started to read Micah's file. He'd intended to before the natural light failed, so he could read without switching on a lamp. It was well into evening now, but he still hadn't turned on the lamp.

He got up and walked warily around the dark apartment. The furniture didn't get rearranged much, so it was no hardship. He knew where he was going anyway.

Milt Kraddock had had this passion for Havana cigars. He had a friend, who had a pal, who knew a guy whose sister lived in Cuba and rolled cigars when she wasn't rolling drunks. Milt hadn't left much behind when he shuffled off this mortal coil, but he had left those fine old Havanas to his colleague.

Sinclair lit one, enjoying the aromatic smoke that curled around his head. A fine smoke, and a fine memory to go with it. Anything else was a gamble.

Luckily, he happened to be a gambling man.

He hefted the file. The Librarian had wanted him to know, to understand. Well, he would certainly try.

He flipped on a lamp stationed alongside his favorite easy chair and transferred himself, plus file, plus burning cigar, into its cozy depths. He neglected to bring an ashtray along, choosing instead to decorate the floor with the respectable remains of the Havana. Some mysterious person connected with the building staff came up twice a week to haul the ashes away and knock the spiderwebs out of the ceiling corners. Sinclair had never met the mysterious person who waged war with the spiders on his behalf and gave his cigar butts decent burials. But then again, to the housekeeping staff, Sinclair was the mysterious tenant who tipped well and went on frequent business trips. And was something of a slob concerning his cigar ash.

Relativity, Sinclair mused, opening the file. How wise Einstein was to insist on its importance. A mystery was only a mystery from the outside looking in. From the inside, it was merely a series of events, someday to be recorded in an innocent-looking file.

He began to read. With each word, his concentration increased, zeroing in on the print, shutting out other sounds, other sensations, until some small portion of his brain registered that the conscious mind of Steve Sinclair was eerily slipping into the role of observer of another man's life.

*   *   *

The following had been carefully clipped from a Biloxi, Mississippi, journal:

April 1969—New Orleans, LA ... The series of "child-ripper" murders continues with the discovery of the body of ten-year-old Madelyn Chartres who disappeared four days ago during the Mardi Gras celebration. The body was found by street vendors in Pirates Alley. Madelyn Chartres is believed to be the sixth victim in a bizarre wave of sex crimes, each preceded by a cryptic note sent to New Orleans police, signed "Capistro."

Inspector Gerard Martin, of the New Orleans Police Department, recipient of the "Capistro" letters, said at a recent press conference," ... 'Capistro' is a seriously deranged individual. He believes himself a reincarnation of Jack the Ripper. The notes I have received are an exact copy, in wording and handwriting, of the notes sent—(allegedly penned by Jack the Ripper)—to London's Central News Agency on September 28, 1888." Inspector Martin offered no explanation of this phenomenon or comment on its bearing in the ongoing child-ripper investigation. Nor would Martin comment on the rumor that the police department, having reached a dead end regarding "Capistro's" true identity, had engaged a psychic in a last desperate attempt ...

"Sweet Jesus!" Inspector Martin howled, burning his tongue on his too-hot black coffee. For good measure, he managed to upset the whole cup on that damn Biloxi paper that was giving him such heartburn. "Manning!" he screamed, sopping ineffectually at the coffee-stained Biloxi journal with a LaFayette daily.

"Yes, sir?" Manning poked his head cautiously through the inspector's door. This Capistro business was making everyone a little short-tempered, and the naturally volatile Martin was practically combustible.

"Help me clean up this mess!" The inspector floundered in his Martin-made coffee swamp as Manning glided forward. Smoothly, he dumped the soaked newsprint into the wastepaper basket. "And who is responsible for this psychobullshit in the papers, eh, Manning?" he snapped.

"Most likely the waiter at Christian's where you lunched with the mayor yesterday afternoon," Manning stated calmly. "You discussed the case with him, didn't you?"

"Idiot! That was the purpose of the luncheon."

"Well ... either you or the mayor must have mentioned a psychic. Most definitely the mayor," Manning amended. Like his fellow officers, Manning personally did not care if the inspector held a seance and raised the spirit of General Lee as long as it put an end to Capistro. He did not want the child-ripper sentenced to death; Manning had already decided a jail term of any duration would be sufficient. He was confident the prison inmates would see to it that Capistro's intestines would shortly decorate the prison exercise yard.

This would not have pleased Inspector Martin. He wanted Capistro's head stuffed and mounted on his office wall. If he could not accomplish that, the mayor wanted the same operation performed on Inspector Martin's head.

"Also ..." Manning interrupted the inspector's train of thought. "The G-man is here."

"FBI?" Martin's eyebrows shot up, crowding his hairline.

"Association." Manning corrected. "Charles Davis, I believe is his name."

"Send him in." The inspector sighed. The big boys were really breathing down his neck on this Capistro psycho case.

Charles Davis entered. He was a big sleepy-faced man, his sharp intellect a hidden weapon behind heavy lids.

"Mr. Davis?" The inspector accepted the huge paw held out to him.

"Better make that Charlie," the Association man rumbled in a low voice. "I might be here awhile."

"Uhh, we appreciate your organization's help," Martin stammered, "but our department is quite capable . . ."

"Of course." Davis waved aside the inspector's discomfort. "I've been dispatched strictly as an observer."

"Observer?" The shoulders went into a casual Gallic shrug. "Standard investigation."

"Is this standard?" The sleepy paw inched its way across Martin's desk and deposited a photocopy of the Biloxi article. "Are you bringing a psychic into this investigation?" He lit a Camel, removed it from his mouth with one hand, picked a fleck of tobacco off his tongue with the other.

Martin watched him glumly. "We are proceeding in the prescribed manner. An investigation of this magnitude takes time and manpower."

The Camel winked fitfully. "The Soviets had a similar problem in sixty. Of course they managed to keep it out of their newspapers."

"The ripper?"

"A ripper. A child molester. Maybe it was Capistro, maybe not. The Soviets aren't talking."

The inspector went through another series of Gallic contortions conveying his nonchalance concerning the entire conversation. "How did the, uh, situation resolve itself?"

"The same way it did in London. The ripper moved on . . . found a new hobby . . . disappeared. But the Soviets redoubled their efforts in psychic research. And naturally"—Charlie inhaled the rest of his cigarette—"the Soviets have been following us pretty closely on this case."

Everybody's watching me, Martin thought miserably.

"They've also been keeping an eye on some of our better-known American psychics," Charlie Davis went on. "My superiors believe that any psychic who can find Capistro is going to win himself a one-way ticket to Mother Russia."

"I see." The inspector bobbed his head, frowning.

"Personally . . ." The agent shook another cigarette out of the pack. "I think this is all a major load of merde, Inspector"—he held out the pack to Martin—"but I have to do what my boss tells me."

Gerard Martin gratefully accepted a Camel and a light, and set about getting his eyebrows back down to where they usually lived. "I am in total agreement with you, Charlie. My boss the mayor told me to contact this psychic; his wife swears by this woman. Her name is Ondine."

Charlie nodded, but this information had already been given him by the Librarian. "When can we see her in action?"

"I've arranged a meeting this afternoon at the Café du Monde," Martin said. "There are some . . . aspects to this case you should know, Charlie." The inspector looked wan. "Some things we've been careful to keep out of the papers, things that would surely cause a panic."

Charlie was beginning to feel a little pale himself. The papers had dutifully recorded the ripper's sexual assaults on his victims and his ceremonial mutilation of their bodies. What else could this monster have done? "What are you talking about, Inspector?"

Martin's voice was thick with disgust and fear. "He smears the blood of his victims on a certain grave marker in the Saint Louis Cemetery number one. It is believed to be the grave of Marie Laveau. Voodoo queen." The inspector watched Charlie Davis's face go blank in disbelief.

"You mean . . ." the agent said slowly. "Capistro killing those children . . . it's like a human sacrifice."

The Café du Monde had only four items on its menu; coffee—with milk or black—milk, hot chocolate, and beignets, the New Orleans improvement over the humble doughnut. Davis and the inspector settled themselves at an outdoor table under the broad awning and waited. Half an hour. Three quarters. The hot Mississippi breeze curdled the milk in Charlie's coffee. Martin had just summoned the waiter to fetch two fresh cups when Ondine finally decided the time was right for her entrance.

The show alone was worth the wait. A tiny woman, Ondine carried herself like a proud queen. She wore a silk dress, actually silk scarves that had been sewn together to decently cover the essential areas of the female anatomy. By the commotion going on under all that silk, it was obvious Ondine had figured the best way to beat the heat

was by eliminating underwear. Long earrings swung
from her lobes, melding into the long flow of near-
jet hair that reached past her waist. Her eyes, a
startling violet, possibly on loan from Elizabeth
Taylor, fastened on Charlie Davis and the inspector.
She swept toward them. In her wake trailed
a twelve-year-old boy, clad in ratty jeans and
sneakers, topped with a baseball undershirt. Under one arm he carried a Batman comic book. His
jaws worked over a huge wad of bubble gum.

"I am here," Ondine announced, gracefully col-
lapsing into a chair. The boy sat down next to her
and devoted his full attention to Batman and
bubble gum.

"Madame." Inspector Martin kissed the psychic's
hand. The Association man settled for a handshake.
Despite her languor, Madame Ondine had a pretty
firm grip.

"It is to find Capistro that you need me, corrrrect?"
Ondine purred. She beckoned to the hovering waiter
and ordered coffee and beignets for herself and the
boy. "Of course this is why; I am psychic, you
know."

"Or you read the papers, madame," the inspector said drily. He offered Ondine a cigarette. She
plucked two from the pack and handed one to the
boy. Charlie, father of four girls, winced. Coffee
and cigarettes for a twelve-year-old.

"Why should I read papers?" Ondine explained
patiently. "I am a psychic person." Their coffee
arrived. Ondine stirred in three spoons of sugar.
The kid took his black, first sticking the wad of
gum to the saucer before he slurped away.

"At any rate," Martin interjected, "we all can

agree that putting an end to this Capistro monster is vital. Madame Ondine . . ."

She waved a hand lazily. "Of course I will help you—"

"Then you agree to undergo testing?"

"Testing?" The silk rustled alarmingly.

"Yes. To"—the inspector searched for a tactful turn of phrase—"validate the authenticity of your psychic gift."

"You think Ondine is a fraud?" Her voice rose. Heads turned throughout the café. "I don't have to listen to this boooooolshit." Majestically, she flounced out of the café and across the street to Jackson Square. The inspector followed imploring, "Madame, madame!"

This left Charlie Davis staring across the table at the Batman devotee. The kid looked up at him. "Mind if I finish my coffee?"

"Help yourself," Charlie said. The kid smiled. One tooth had come in crooked and was crowding his lower jaw. Braces, Charlie Davis, father of four, thought automatically. "You got a name, kid?"

"Micah."

"Charlie." They shook hands solemnly. "How's Batman doing?"

The kid shrugged. "Ah, same old stuff. You know." Charlie Davis allowed as he did. "You think my mother's a phony?"

"I didn't say that."

" 'Cause you guys aren't doing that great a job. You should beg her to help you."

"Well . . ." the agent said. "It looked kind of bad, her flying off the handle at the mention of testing."

"She could help you," the kid insisted.

Nice, Charlie thought, a loyal kid. "You like baseball?"

Micah brightened. "Sure. Mets are gonna take the pennant this year."

At that moment, the Mets were in spring training, somewhere in Florida. "Did your mother tell you that?"

"Mets are gonna take it," the kid said unconcernedly. "Sure wish I could see that."

Charlie grinned. He loved his four girls but he had always wanted a boy. "Maybe you and your mom will come east for the World Series."

"She don't like baseball."

"I'll take you."

"Yeah?" Micah rolled up the comic and stuffed it into a back pocket. He drained his coffee cup and stood. "Okay, Charlie, you got a deal." He frowned. "What's an 'eee-chan'?"

Charlie Davis felt his short hairs stand on end. "I have four daughters. No sons. We can't have any more children. So my wife got me a little dog, a little male dog. We kid around, call him our first son. Ii-chan is Japanese for first son. That's the dog's name." Ii-chan.

"Oh," the kid said. "I was wondering."

Before Charlie could say another word, Micah had melted into the crowd, Batman waving jauntily from one hip pocket.

Charlie was paying the bill when he felt a tug at his sleeve. He looked down. "Hey sport, why'd you take off so fast?"

"You have to come with me," Micah said. The desperation in his voice was genuine, there was no mistaking that.

"Hang on a minute, son—"

"No. Now!" He flopped, throwing his full weight onto the sleeve. With some irritation, Charlie noted his shoulder seam was going. "Okay, okay. Lead on, Macduff."

"Is this it?" The agent looked around in amazement. Micah had taken him to an elementary school.

"Shhh." The kid sat down and waited. In a few minutes, the dismissal bell rang and children began to pour out of the huge double doors into the enclosed courtyard. "Okay. Look for a girl in a red corduroy jumper," Micah instructed him. The courtyard activity began to boil over into the street. Kids swinging lunch boxes: Fred Flintstone, Barbie . . . Barbie keeping company with chubby pink legs peeping out from under a red jumper.

"Hi, Elyse." Micah fell in with the troupe of giggling fifth-grade girls. Charlie trailed at some distance, confused and wary.

Red jumper goggled at the raggedy boy. "How do you know my name?"

"Ah, I just know it," Micah said. "Can I walk you home?" All the little girls giggled anew.

"My mother told me not to talk to strangers," little Elyse said primly. She and her cohorts clattered away.

"Is that your little girlfriend?" Charlie inquired.

"You saw her?" The boy began to pace distractedly.

"Yes."

"You saw her. You know what she looks like. Her name's Elyse, Elyse Halloran. Remember that."

A nasty thought crossed the agent's mind. The kid was either on drugs or emotionally disturbed.

"You don't believe me." He stopped pacing and

stared at Charlie mournfully. Starving orphan on the next to last page of the Sunday news magazine. "I thought if I told you about Ii-chan you would believe me." His shoulders drooped tiredly.

"Believe what?" Charlie said helplessly. They were both standing still, but Charlie could feel the boy drifting away from him.

"I've done all I can." He seemed smaller and younger than he had in the café. "I found Elyse Halloran and I took you to her. You have to look after her now." He sat down on the curb, shivering. Charlie sat next to him.

"Why do we have to look after Elyse?" he said gently.

"You know." The boy seemed close to tears. "She's next."

Charlie Davis spent his evening making phone calls.

He called Inspector Martin and advised Martin of his afternoon's adventures with Ondine's boy. Martin advised that he thought Ondine's boy was quietly off his rocker. Elyse Halloran was obviously some little heartbreaker the boy was trying to impress.

Charlie Davis called his boss, the Librarian, and advised him of same. The Librarian digested this and told Charlie to "keep him appraised of further developments." No manpower could be spared to guard the Halloran child; nor did the Librarian feel such action was necessary.

Charlie Davis called his wife and inquired after the health of his dog. After she stopped laughing, his wife told him yes, the dog was fine and she and the girls were okay, too.

Charlie Davis did not call Mr. and Mrs. Halloran. He did not know where they lived and there were many Hallorans in the phone directory. He felt it would be wrong to alarm them.

Still, he was not all that surprised when Inspector Martin called bright and early the next morning to tell him Elyse Halloran had made history as Capistro's seventh victim.

"Why are you holding that kid?" Charlie bellowed, landing a large fist on the inspector's desk. "Do you really think a twelve-year-old is physically capable of such a crime?"

Martin was unflappable. "He is a strong boy. You yourself expressed a belief he might be emotionally disturbed or under the influence of a controlled substance."

"But he's twelve years old! At least send him over to Juvenile Hall. You've got him locked up with real criminals."

Manning appeared. "Mr. Davis? Message for you." He handed Charlie a folded slip of paper.

Must speak to you. Interrogation Room six.
                                        Ondine

She was chewing at her nails when he got there. Her outlandish costume of the previous afternoon had been exchanged for low-slung blue jeans and a Tulane T-shirt. Forest green. It did wild things to her violet eyes.

"He didn't do it," she began, gratefully accepting the offered cigarette.

"I know." He flicked his lighter and she bent over the quivering flame. "Tell the truth, Ondine, you couldn't predict the weather. It's the kid, isn't it?"

She nodded, exhaling a jet of dirty smoke. "If you've got the time, I've got a very short biography."

"I've got time."

"We're from Lafayette. Cajun Country. His father was a Cajun farmer. We weren't married. He already had a wife." Her narrative was terse, emotionless. "My family allowed me to stay until my child was born, then I moved to the city and managed as well as any other woman who has no skills besides her looks. About a year ago, Micah told me a friend's house was going to burn. She wouldn't believe him. So he said I had told him."

"Then she listened?"

"Yes."

"And the place burned?"

"To the ground." She stubbed out the cigarette. "After that, my reputation was made. People just started coming to me."

"He did the work and you took the applause," Charlie translated.

"It wasn't that way," she said earnestly. "I didn't want people to look at him like a freak."

"But you can take it."

"Please try to understand what I'm saying." In her jeans and T-shirt, she could have been a co-ed passionately declaring her allegiance to some cause. "You think it's some kind of a gift. It's not!" She laughed hoarsely. "You have to pay for it. With your privacy . . . people never leave you alone. I thought it would be nice if he had a childhood. Me"—her slim shoulders shrugged—"I'm used to people staring, calling names after me in the street."

She looked at him defiantly. "I know who I am and what I've been."

"They'll have to release him, Ondine," Charlie tried to comfort her. "Martin doesn't have any evidence."

"But the damage may already be done."

"He'll get over it," Charlie upheld staunchly. "And when Martin releases him, don't get defensive on me now, I'd like Micah to undergo some testing. We still have a lunatic to catch."

Ondine was still pensive. "He'll do whatever you ask him to do; he likes you."

"You don't sound very happy."

She accepted another cigarette and stared at the pyramid on the Camel box. "I'm his mother, tried to be a good one. Now my kid's locked up in jail—"

"It's not in the papers." Charlie tried to keep his voice level. "When it's all over, you will help him, good mother that you are, accept the things that are happening in his life now. Will you sign the consent forms for the tests?"

Ondine nodded. "Yes." She hesitated, one hand on the doorknob. "I've been honest with you, I haven't got a psychic bone in my body."

Charlie grinned. "Me neither. It's no sin."

"Still . . ." She frowned, dark hair curtaining her shoulders and back.

"I understand." Charlie laughed uneasily. "I've got a bad feeling about this, too. It's a good thing neither one of us is psychic."

That night Capistro went on date number eight. Micah, enjoying the hospitality of the police department, had an airtight alibi. Inspector Martin rang Charlie Davis's hotel room to tell him the news.

There was no answer. Charlie Davis was sleeping with Ondine in her apartment.

When Micah was released the next morning he took one look at Charlie, one look at his mother, and he knew. Psychic or not, he just knew.

"Okay, kid." Charlie ruffled Micah's hair while the kid looked up at him suspiciously. "Ready for some tests?"

"Sure, Charlie." He stopped staring down Davis and tried withering Ondine with a icy gaze. She reached out and gave him a little swat on the rear. He cooled out and obediently followed the technician to the testing area.

"What now?" Ondine asked.

"Now, we wait for the test results." He patted her hand reassuringly, and her fingers interlocked with his gracefully. Inspector Martin watched them and said nothing.

Four hours later, the rattled technician threw a stack of mimeographed notes down on Inspector Martin's desk. Charlie Davis, sitting in a chair tipped up against the wall, snapped forward so quickly the chair did a solo boogie before calming itself. The two men sifted through the notes. Scientific gobledygook.

Martin's eyebrows dueled with his hairline again. "Can we get a translation?"

"Yeah, sure." The technician nodded jerkily. "He hits ninety percent of the time."

Charlie shot to his feet. "Ninety-percent accuracy?"

"Yeah, but we could have caught him on a bad

day," the tech explained. "It may not last all his adult life, either. See, usually ESP is a recessive gene, a wild-card trait. This kid is the first in his family to display any psychic ability"—he held up a hand—"that we know of. At ninety-percent accuracy I'd say he'd tip over as a psychic within five to six years."

"Tip over?"

"Dry up. No more ESP," the tech said. "Of course he could learn some new tricks by then. Telekenesis, teleportation, shit, maybe even parthenogenesis. We could have something interesting here."

"Or a fluke."

"Yeah, total fluke." This prospect did not seem to calm the tech any.

"In your opinion," Charlie asked, "do you think this kid could locate Capistro?"

The tech nodded slowly. Charlie turned to the inspector.

Martin sighed. "I suppose we have no choice, no other leads, no other hope."

"Okay." The tech headed for the door. "I'll give him a copy of *Playboy*, that should keep him busy till you need him."

Charlie stood squarely in his path. "Gentlemen, let's try to remember the subject is a minor. His involvement in this case should be kept confidential." He knew the inspector wouldn't be a problem; Martin was deeply embarrassed that a psychic had been brought into his investigation, let alone a twelve-year-old. Charlie was worried about the tech. The tech also swore not to tell a soul, but he assumed his wife was not included in that group. The tech's wife told no one but her first cousin Rose, whom she was very close to, like sisters they were. Cousin Rose told only the cashier in the coffee shop of the Hilton, where she was employed as a waitress. The cashier was like a daughter to her. The cashier told her boyfriend. The boyfriend said he did not care that the cops had called in a twelve-year-old psychic to find Capistro the child-ripper. But he told a friend in his office anyway. Just to make small talk.

"Francis DePaul," Micah announced decisively.

"Are you sure?" Charlie looked at the three photographs on the table. With Micah's help, they'd boiled the choices down to three possible suspects, all with clean records. Not so much as a parking ticket. If the kid was wrong, they were going to hear some major-league citizen squawking.

"Yeah, it's DePaul all right. He's Capistro." He sighed. "Phew. Is this over? Can I go home now?"

Martin snagged the picture, scanned the thumbnail bio on the back, printed over the "Kodak paper" mark. "Postal clerk. I don't know, it's like the butler did it. Too obvious."

"Can't be too obvious; you didn't think of it." Micah drummed wipeout on the table top. "DePaul's the guy. What do you do now? Get a search warrant, huh?"

"Yes. I don't suppose you'd have the address?" the inspector mused.

Micah grimaced. "Jeez, I gotta do everything?" He grinned at Charlie. "Bet I'd make a good cop, huh?" Charlie laughed. A great cop. He'd wind up shooting anyone who was even thinking about pulling a gun. "We still on for the World Series, Charlie?"

"Sure, kid."

"Good," Micah said innocently. "I bet Mom would like to meet Mrs. Davis."

Inspector Martin giggled, made a manful attempt to stifle it, wound up tearing at the eyes. He left, tearing and giggling.

"I want to go with you," Micah said. His hands were quiet on the table. "When you get DePaul."

"No," Charlie said firmly. "If he is Capistro, it's better if he knows nothing about you and your mother." He tousled the kid's dark hair. "Relax. I'll tell you all about it when the shooting's over."

From a particular point of view, Charlie thought, you could say Francis DePaul was being cooperative. He wasn't home. Martin's men did a rather discreet B and E and shouldered their way into the sad little apartment.

Charlie found himself staring at DePaul's meager bookshelves. Martin was right, the whole thing was obvious. In the midst of a few cheap paperbacks (H. P. Lovecraft and porn) were a few very expensive volumes: two on Jack the Ripper, one lovingly bound copy of *Gray's Anatomy*, a Satanic Bible with a glittering silver-gilt edge.

"Too easy," he murmured, that nasty feeling on his spine again.

"Inspector?" An officer came out of DePaul's bedroom carrying a shoe box. "The bastard kept souvenirs. Look, a hair ribbon . . . all kinds of stuff."

"I think we have enough here to hang DePaul." The inspector tried to keep the loathing out of his clipped voice.

"What are you doing in my house?" All heads spun to the door. DePaul was home. He was surprisingly young and handsome. In his post office uniform he looked like the hero in a World War II flick. He took one look at the open shoebox and tried to run. In a flash, two cops grabbed him and did their best to discourage him from trying that again. DePaul erupted into a screaming maniac. Two more cops leaped in. It took the four of them to hustle DePaul downstairs to a patrol car.

The inspector clapped Charlie on the shoulder. "It's over, my friend. Thank God, it's finally over."

DePaul was getting nervous. He knew what he'd done wrong; he'd neglected to make the final blood sacrifice to Marie LaVeau. The voodoo queen had told him the secrets of Jack the Ripper. DePaul had dared to think he could evade capture without her help.

Helpless, handcuffed in the back of a patrol car, two armed officers riding up front, Francis DePaul breathed a silent prayer to the voodoo queen. She answered him.

He began to choke.

One of the officers in the front seat turned around. "Hey, pull over!" he called to the driver. "This guys choking, maybe we hit him on the larynx. Pull over!" The officer bent over DePaul, loosening his shirt and tie. DePaul jammed both thumbs into the officer's eyes and propelled him backward into the driver. As the car spun out of control DePaul slammed the door level and was thrown out onto the street. The police car hit an embankment and flipped over. Gravity tugged at the blinded officer; he slithered out the front window. DePaul cautiously walked over, grabbed the officer's gun and the handcuff key. The driver was dead.

DePaul knelt by the blinded offier; cocked the

gun. "Gotta hurt bad, man. Tell me who put the finger on me and I'll see to it you get to a hospital."

The officer sobbed.

"Who?"

"Ondine."

DePaul promptly shot him in the head, leaving the young officer with three bloody holes where his face had been.

Charlie Davis wept when he saw what DePaul had done to Ondine. She lay on a slab in the morgue, a sheet draped around her.

DePaul had sexually assaulted her. He had carved the word "whore" across her chest. He had savaged her long hair; some of it had been cut off, some ripped away with bits of her scalp.

"What happened to the boy?" Charlie asked tight-lipped.

"Gone," the inspector answered. "Vanished."

"Just like Capistro," Charlie reminded him.

Micah was half asleep in the back of a panel truck. There were a lot of blankets, so it was okay. The men who put him there gave him something to make him sleep, which was good because he didn't really want to think just that minute. Until he could sort things out, he figured to stay with those men.

But the little voice that told him things—told him DePaul was Capistro, told him not to go home to be murdered like his mother—that voice told him not to stay with these men too long. His friend Charlie would not like these men. Somehow it was important to get back to Charlie.

"We're quite positive the KGB has him," the Librarian's voice crackled through the telephone receiver. "We've been monitoring their radio transmissions. He's unharmed."

"Won't they try to get him out of the country?" Charlie asked.

"We'll make sure they are unable to accomplish that."

"How, sir?"

"Details," the Librarian said negligently. "Details."

A panel truck pulled into a gas station. A man looking a little wilted in his business suit let a boy out of the back of the truck. Together they walked to the men's room.

"It's locked!" the owner yelled out to them. They weren't any of the usual truckers, so the owner was a little nervous. He'd been held up often enough to keep an automatic Remington rifle by the cash register.

Yes, sir, old Remmy would take care of him.

He gave the washroom key to the man and watched him let the kid into the can. A minute or so later the kid came out. The man put his arm around the boy and steered him back to the truck.

"Hey, my key! Give me my key back!"

The kid got out of the cab with the key in his hand, walking to the register. "Sorry, mister." He smiled. He had a tooth coming in a little crooked.

The owner softened as soon as he got his key back. "That's okay, sonny . . ." Without warning, the kid swooped, grabbed the Remmy, and opened fire on the cab of the panel truck.

They never even had a chance to shoot back.

When he was through, Micah leaned the gun back against the register.

"Russian spies," he explained to the owner. "The American spies are waiting for me down the highway, about five miles." The man backed away from him. "They'll come and clean up the mess."

"Sure, kid." The owner edged back further. "Just don't hurt me, okay?" He didn't breath a sigh of relief till the kid was out of sight, hiking down the road.

He hiked about five miles down the highway till he came to the Lucky Clover Truckstop where Charlie Davis was having a cup of coffee prior to going down the highway and rescuing Micah.

Micah let himself into the unlocked car and snapped on the radio. He waited patiently. Charlie paid his bill, went out to the parking area, and got the biggest shock of his life.

"Hi," Micah said. "I shot those KGB guys and left them in their truck at this gas station up the road. You better straighten it out with the owner." He changed radio stations, settling on the Beatles. "I'm beat. Take me someplace where I can sleep for a year." He finally noticed Charlie was in shock. "Well aren't you glad to see me?"

"I didn't see nothing," the gas station owner protested to Charlie Davis. Behind them, Association men were quietly picking up the KGB boys with tweezers and blotters. "All I know is I don't ever want to see that kid again. That is a scary kid."

Charlie shrugged. "He's just a kid, mister. It's the situation that's . . . unusual."

"Yeah? Wish he was yours?" A few days ago, Charlie's answer would have been yes. Now . . .

The owner laughed. "That's what I thought. Yessir, that's one scary kid."

Charlie looked back at his car. Micah had the window rolled down and he was watching the forensic team cart away the bodies. Charlie got in the car.

"What's the difference," Micah asked without looking at him, "between their guys and your guys?"

"Let's just say there is a difference," Charlie said. He put the car in gear. It bucked a little. "You can believe me, there's a difference."

Charlie Davis spent the rest of his life trying to teach Micah the difference. At the moment of his death, he still felt unassured of his success.

Capistro was never apprehended.

*   *   *

Steve Sinclair tried to dig himself out of his favorite easy chair without disturbing the interesting pattern the cigar ash had formed on his chest and stomach. After a while, he gave up, let the ashes fall wherever they wanted, and got himself a beer.

He read the rest of the file standing up, because there wasn't much left and his right foot had fallen asleep. The rest was the kind of stuff he was expecting . . . a stint in a mental institution, under the guise of "observation" (two years), expanding to an out-patient program, and finally, joining the Association at age nineteen with the blessings of God, the Librarian, and Charlie Davis. As that tech had predicted, Micah's ESP talent did disappear, resurfacing in a slightly altered form: mental dominance.

The last item in the file was a standard report on Charles Davis's death, two weeks prior. He had died quietly, at home, in bed, of a stroke. Charlie was never one to cause a fuss. He was survived by a wife, four daughters, and an arthritic dachshund named Ii-chan.

The phone rang. "Sinclair here."

"Steve?" The Librarian's voice sounded very near.

"Yes, sir."

"I've taken the liberty of reserving you a ticket on Thai Airlines, flight four-nineteen, at ten tomorrow morning. Of course you may use it at your own discretion, the choice is yours." He hung up.

"You old bastard." Sinclair laughed. "You knew I'd go." But just this once, he amended. He had no intention of baby-sitting some looney-tunes agent until he decided to reach his emotional maturity.

Still feeling pretty awake, Sinclair lit another cigar, turned out the light, and settled back in his favorite chair.

It met all the criteria to be a favorite chair: it was old, scarred, and didn't match anything else in the whole apartment. The only thing it matched was old cigar ash. Sinclair loved that chair. He wondered if Micah had a favorite chair or just threw everything out the window when it outlived its usefulness.

"Okay, Micah," he said to the darkness. "I'll hang out, see how you do without Charlie holding your hand." The plain truth was Sinclair was a team player from the word "go."

Kraddock, Mitchell, Anderson; they'd been the best.

With a pang, Sinclair realized they were slowly fading, relegated to the part of his mind reserved for memories; back there with old schoolteachers and old lovers. The smell of a good hand-rolled Havana.

Not Amanda, though. Somehow, she would always live for him; that was right, and part of him hoped Micah had not destroyed his memory of lovely, noble Ondine.

But the old F.S. Force; he was slowly getting over it. He was ready to fight again. He walked to the kitchen, carrying the file, and took it to the sink. With a smile, he touched the glowing ash of Kraddock's cigar to Micah's file; a passing of torches.

When it was all burned up, he ran water in the sink till it was clean and went to bed.

He slept like a baby.

chapter 9

"Trans-International Airlines flight number four-nineteen is now boarding at gate thirty-two," crooned a silky female voice over the airport loudspeaker. "Passengers in nonsmoking rows sixty to eighty may now line up for seating."

Sinclair scanned the terminal again. No sign of Micah. He stood up, stretched, and got in line.

Directly in front of him an enterprising young student was diligently punching away at a pocket calculator. Probably figuring out the frequency with which those big birds made unscheduled landings, usually nose first. The price you pay for flying first class.

"Surprise, surprise." He heard an amused voice behind him. Micah. If the last of the Mohicans had been able to creep around as quietly as Micah, there'd probably be a few more around today. Discreetly, Sinclair shot a look down at the Cajun's feet. Keds. White hightops.

"Have you reenlisted?" Micah asked.

"Limited hitch." They got their seat assignments and headed for gate thirty-two.

"What changed your mind?"

Sinclair laughed softly. "Must be your charming personality."

"Huh." Micah seemed unconvinced.

Son of a gun, Sinclair thought; he knows something's up. The agent resolved to do some quiet research on psychic phenomena.

A buxom stewardess extended a slim hand. "Tickets, please." Her orange-painted nails plucked the tickets from Sinclair's hand, fingers resting on his a little longer than necessary.

"I'm a leg man myself," Micah said as they approached their seats.

The green cushioned chairs were three abreast. The window seat of the row assigned to Micah and Sinclair was occupied by Jez Cooke. Her coltish legs were crossed at the knee; her face wore a wry expression.

"Good morning, gentlemen." She pulled a gray envelope out of the elasticized pocket on the seat in front of her and handed it to Sinclair. "Or should I say welcome aboard?"

Micah frowned. "What are you doing here?"

"The Librarian has . . . what is the expression, enlisted my services. I have . . . skills. Skills that are appropriate for this job. At least the Librarian thinks so. It's all in my dossier." She nodded in Sinclair's direction.

Micah made no attempt to hide his disbelief, or his disapproval. "You mean we're working on this assignment together?"

"That's right." She looked down at her seat belt. "Listen. This is very difficult for me to say. I'm sorry about the way I acted yesterday. My sister and I . . ." She ran her fingers slowly through her long red hair. "We were very close. I can't believe she was mixed up with drugs. I have to know the truth."

Sinclair squeezed her hand warmly, by way of support. She looked up at him. Her eyes had the same determined, intelligent expression that he remembered so clearly from their meeting the previous day. Not all of that casual cool had been a put-on. Just some of it.

She pulled Tina's last letter out of her purse and handed it to Sinclair. "When I got home from the spa yesterday, I found this."

"From Tina?"

She nodded. "Look at the postmark."

"April sixth."

"The day they found her body."

Micah couldn't pretend he was uninterested any longer. "What's in it?"

She gave them both a Cheshire Cat smile and said, "You're the experts, you tell me."

While Micah and Sinclair read the letter, Jez settled back to watch the in-flight movie. It was a James Bond film, *On Her Majesty's Secret Service*, with Diana Rigg, and as 007, George Lazenby, the Bond whose name no one could remember.

Jez was sure she was going to enjoy it.

Richard D'Arbanville was riding in the back of his air-conditioned limousine, on his way to Bangkok International Airport. He poured himself a tall glass of Chivas Regal over one cube of ice.

All that disturbed his feeling exquisite tranquillity was the relentlessly droning voice of Lieutenant Juan Valjenos, who was holding forth on his favorite topic: himself. In fact, that's why D'Arbanville opted for a tall glass of scotch.

"So you see, Lord D., I do have the situation entirely under control. As I told you before, your visit was unnecessary."

D'Arbanville did not allow smoking in the limo, but Valjenos seemed to believe he was enjoying one of his precious imported cigars, as he liked to whenever he was expounding his philosophies of life. He blew an imaginery jet of cigar smoke, and continued. "There are only two things these people with whom we deal understand: force, and money."

D'Arbanville, mellowed by cocaine and alcohol, was amused rather than annoyed by the Argentinian's cockiness. "You do not consider three messy deaths in the space of a week a rather alarming statistic?"

Valjenos's answer was an indifferent shrug.

D'Arbanville took a gulp of his drink and rolled it around like mouthwash before swallowing. It burned deliciously as it went down. "If you survive in this business as long as I have, my dear boy, you will learn that such surface trouble is only an indication of an iceberg of chaos and unrest beneath the surface."

Valjenos threw back his head and laughed heartily. "Sir, I truly enjoy the way you talk, but in reality it is only so much cowshit. Tina Cooke was not a member of the organization and so not our problem. Sammy Wuan was basically a drifter who tomorrow will be forgotten like the news. Gogee Loo was a nobody, easily replaced, who will serve as an example, a reminder to any other employees who contemplate stepping out of line." Valjenos's voice and manner turned suddenly sly and conspiratorial. "Besides, if you really believed as you say, you would not so calmly leave Bangkok, now, eh?"

You stupid oaf, thought D'Arbanville. I take the money and you take the fall. Aloud he said, "Ah, you are right, Juan. I do admire the way you . . . control things here. We are the perfect partnership. You the iron hand, I the velvet glove."

"Yes, that is us." Valjenos blew imaginary smoke rings. "The iron hand." He thrust his fist upward in a power salute. "The velvet glove," he whispered admiringly.

The limousine stopped directly in front of the airport entrance. D'Arbanville did not like to walk.

Ling, who was driving the limo, informed them that they had reached their destination. "Should I take your luggage up for you, Lord D'Arbanville?"

"Well, it's not going to walk there by itself, now is it?"

Ling wasn't sure whether this was a joke or not. After knocking it around in his head for a minute, he laughed, just to be on the safe side.

D'Arbanville finished his drink in one long swallow. He handed Valjenos the empty glass and pressed a button in the armrest. The black-tinted glass of his window slowly descended, letting in bright sunlight and the sights and sounds of the busy airport.

In the distance, D'Arbanville spied a familiar form. He leaned closer, disbelieving. Squinting through the sunlight to get a better look, he recognized the broad shoulders, but . . .

"Is something the matter, Lord D.?" Valjenos inquired loudly.

"Shut up, you idiot!"

Valjenos was flabbergasted. "But, Lord D."

"Hand me your binoculars. Now."

His tone meant business. Valjenos complied, wordlessly.

As he lifted the binoculars to his eyes, D'Arbanville shook his head in amazement and admiration. One quick look was all he needed for confirmation. His lips formed the name, Steven Sinclair; his voice let out a long almost soundless growl.

Ling opened the door to the limo. "We're all set, Lord D'Arbanville. Your bags are being checked right now."

"Get them back. Put them in the trunk. Then drive me back to the hotel. I'm staying in Bangkok for a while." His voice was flat and expressionless. His eyes never left Sinclair. His right hand affectionately rubbed the pet he wore on his left little finger.

Valjenos and Ling exchanged a puzzled look. Both men knew better than to argue.

chapter 10

Jez had insisted on carrying her own luggage into the Embassy Hotel. Just to prove to these two guys what a hip, together kind of lady she was. By the time she reached the elevator she realized it was going to take a lot more than a pointless display of female muscle to impress these boys.

Both Sinclair and Micah (did he have a last name, Jez wondered, or was he just terribly informal?) had been studying her, discreetly of course, since they'd boarded the plane. And she'd been watching them (after savoring Lazenby's exploits as Bond).

Micah did crossword puzzles. In ink. Quickly. Accurately? Jez wondered about that, too. He soon tired of this and plugged his ears with the swimming pool–blue plastic earphones the airline supplied for a nominal fee. He spun the channel dial on the armrest. Curious, Jez spun along to the channel Micah had selected. Mozart. She'd figured him for a Wagner man. In the next five minutes, he checked out every channel the airline offered.

Jez gave up following him and flipped on the country-western channel. Hoyt Axton sing-talking about a cat named Kalamazoo. Jez had been to Kalamazoo. She thought the cat should speedily set about getting a new name.

Bored, she turned her head. Sinclair was staring right into her eyes. One of those little freak things, he'd looked up from his magazine just as she'd turned her head. He smiled absently, but it took a moment before the message to act pleasant went from conscious mind to mouth muscles. Jez smiled back, but for a second her whole being went "Arghhh!" Steve Sinclair did not like this amateur tagging along on his mission. She looked down to see what he was reading. *Psychology Today.*

"Terrific," Jez muttered.

"Did you say something?" Sinclair came out of his magazine, studying her as though she were truly something fascinating, like an albino cockroach with young.

"Huh, what?" Micah said, slipping the earphones down around his neck.

"Nothing." Jez slapped her forehead, exasperated, feeling like a total jerk.

"Nervous?" Micah's hand grazed hers on their mutual armrest.

"A little," she admitted. "Fear of the unknown, you know."

"Ahhh." Sinclair nodded sagely, deeply involved in *Psychology Today.*

"Relax." Micah smiled at her.

She smiled back, but something bothered her. A little nagging something at the back of her mind. For some insane reason her brain conjured up an image of a snake charmer. "I guess you guys have done this hundreds of times." She couldn't shake the picture.

"You guessed right."

"How long have you two been working together?" she asked.

"This is our first assignment as a team," Sinclair answered her. "So we are all the new kid on the block, so to speak."

"Oh," Jez said politely. There was that goddamn snake charmer again. With an effort, she pushed the image out of her mind. Sinclair saw Micah sit back in his chair and rub his temple. Something happened there, Sinclair told himself.

"Would you excuse me? I've got to stretch my legs or I'll die." Jez squeezed past and sauntered up the narrow aisle, pausing at the stewardess's jumpseat to look out the window.

"Did you try something with Miss Cooke?" Sinclair asked his new partner.

Micah was still rubbing his forehead. "Yeah. I tried to give her a mental command. Something easy, go to sleep."

Jez was chatting with one of the stewardesses.

"Looks wide-awake to me," Sinclair observed. "Must be tougher than she looks."

The Cajun nodded. "Strong-willed. Intuitive. She knew I was trying to push her. Maybe not consciously, but she sensed something. That's why she suddenly had to go stretch her legs." He thought a moment. "Either that or we're not as adorable as we thought we were."

"Speak for yourself." Sinclair grinned.

"Yup," Micah mused. "Strong-willed, intuitive, a black belt . . . everything a man could wish for. Sooo . . . why am I not happy she's here?"

"Fear of the unknown," Sinclair said. "We don't know her, we don't know each other . . ." and, he added silently, we aren't really sure the Librarian hasn't made the first mistake of his career assembling this crew. The senior agent watched Micah observing the pretty redhead. Something occurred to him. ". . . and she's one of the two kinds of women you cannot sleep with."

Micah looked at him, curiously. "Now I don't agree with you, but I must say you've got my curiosity piqued. Pray tell, what are these two kinds of women?"

"Women you work with . . ." Sinclair said promptly.

"And?"

"Friends' sisters." Sinclair selected an article on schizophrenia and the performing arts. "Oh, by the way, Micah," he said softly. "I trust you know enough not to try your little party trick on me." He turned the page carefully. "Because if you do, and I catch you at it, and rest assured I will, you will find yourself on a liquid diet for a long, long time."

Micah's smile faded. "When this is over, Stevie boy, let's you and me take a meeting. Your choice of weapons."

"I don't need any help taking you apart, kid."

"Your two friends," the stewardess was saying to Jez, "so good looking."

"Uh-huh."

"And you know what I really like?" the stewardess gushed. "They get along so well."

Jez grinned. "That's just what I was thinking."

Before she had time to adjust, Jez found herself schlepping her suitcases into Room 1605 of the Embassy Hotel, tired, dirty, and just a tad cranky. To make matters worse, there'd been a slight screw-up at the desk. Micah and Sinclair's rooms, 1601 and 1603, were not ready yet. The harried clerk promised to ring them in 1605 when the other rooms had been made up.

Disgusted and weary, they all trooped into 1605. Micah slumped in a chair, legs stretched out in front of him. His face wore a smoking-in-the-boys'-room look. Sinclair's expression was, as usual, unreadable. He sat on the edge of the bed, feet flat, spine straight.

The phone rang. "I'll get it," Sinclair announced. He stumbled over Micah's feet, directly in his path. "That's it! You need to learn some manners ... now!"

"Suits me fine," Micah snarled, leaping to his feet, peeling off his jacket. Resisting the temptation to smack Micah in the teeth right then, Sinclair started taking off his jacket. Just as he flung it aside, his outstretched arm was grabbed. By Jezebel.

Expertly, she threw him into one wall and, scarcely taking a breather, chucked Micah into the opposite wall. They both lumbered to their feet, belligerence transformed to astonishment. Jez stood between them, poised for another exhibition of Dr. Tanaka's teachings. The phone, receiving no attention, gave up and shut up.

"Still feel like fighting, boys?" she threatened.

"Nooo." Micah rubbed the back of his head, which had gone into the wall first.

"So much for the juvenile delinquent." She turned to Sinclair. "What about older-but-not-wiser?"

"What the hell . . ." Sinclair said sheepishly, offering up his hand.

Micah grasped it. "Why not?" His eyes held a playful glint. "We can always kill each other at a more opportune moment. After the mission."

"After," Sinclair agreed. For the moment, the situation was defused.

The phone rang again. Jez stretched across the bed and snagged it.

"Your rooms are ready, thank God," she said, tugging the pillow out from the tight bedclothes. She slipped it under her head and stared up at the ceiling. "Why are we all here?" she moaned.

Micah looked back at her, surprised. "I don't know about you guys, but I happen to like my job." He dragged his luggage out the door.

"Y'know," Jez said lazily. "he's either very well adjusted or just a touch crazy." She vaulted off the bed lightly and retrieved Sinclair's jacket from the floor, where it had been looking terribly lonely. "As it stands, I'm leaning more toward crazy. Still . . ." She sighed, automatically folding his jacket. "I suppose he's a good agent. He just looks so young." She was still folding.

Sinclair rescued his jacket. "He's been an agent since he was nineteen."

She reflected. "Maybe that's why he's crazy."

He smiled.

A sad smile, Jez thought. "You don't talk much."

He nodded in agreement.

She laughed. "And I talk too much."

"Amounts to the same thing."

"Sometimes."

"Sometimes." He looped the jacket over one arm, extended the other toward her. Her grip was firm

and dry. No temerity. "I'm beginning to understand why the Librarian insisted on you joining
the team."

Jez smiled. "I'm the referee." Her soft voice was
a benediction.

"Uh-huh." He realized he was still holding her
hand and let go. "Tomorrow we'll take in the sights,
get our Thai legs, so to speak. Good night."

"Good night."

"Oh, one more thing," Sinclair said. "You want
to watch out for little Mr. Micah."

"I can fend off a pass pretty well."

"You don't understand." He frowned; how exactly do I put this? "He's what's referred to as a
mental dominant." He thought of *Psychology Today* buried someplace in his gear. "I think I have
an article that explains—"

"Snake charmer." She swore softly. Even Sinclair had to admire her choice of adjectives. Maybe
it had to do with being a Texan.

"Exactly. Well forewarned . . ."

"Thanks. A little late . . . but thanks." She slipped
off one shoe, stared at its mate, a hundred questions on her face.

He sensed her waiting for him to ask, so he did.
"Something on your mind?"

"I was just thinking," she said in that voice he
was beginning to get used to. "What a sad collec-
tion of the walking wounded we are. Do you really
think we can do it?"

He thought of D'Arbanville out there, waiting
for them. A very dangerous man. Sinclair wasn't
sure they could do it, he only knew they had to.
"Yes, Jez. I think you can do it."

"Thank you for that." She grinned, head cocked to one side. "Hey. Get well soon, partner."

"You, too."

She slipped off the other shoe. "Feel better already." He let himself out quietly.

Jez quickly shed her clothes, digging out her favorite sleeping gear, one of Dad's old shirts. For once in her life she'd had the foresight to pack it on top of all the other crap in her suitcase.

She had just buttoned up when there was a knock at her door. "Steve?"

It was Micah, balancing a tray on his fingertips like a career waiter. He looked inside her room, though he did not step past the doorway. "Is he beating my time already? Thought you might like some tea."

"Is that a coy way to invite yourself in?" she said suspiciously.

"Check it out, sugar." His entire manner changed to that of a street hawker. "One cup, see?" Then he became an English butler. "One lump or two?"

Amazing, Jez thought. A one-man show. Or a very personable schizophrenic. She leaned against the doorframe. "Anyone ever tell you that you have the personality of a speed freak?"

"Flatterer. Uh . . . I sort of owe you an apology. . . ."

"Yeah," Jez said drily. "I know all about your little trick. I'll forgive you this time."

"My fatal charm getting to you, huh?"

She collapsed against the doorframe, convulsed with laughter. "Jet lag is getting to me. I can't keep up with you."

"Savoir-faire is everywhere." He imitated a cartoon voice that sounded vaguely familiar.

"Savoir-faire?"

"Nemesis of Klondike Kat. Little mouse that went around in an airplane."

"New Orleans!" she cried out delightedly. "I was trying to place the accent. At first I thought it was Brooklyn."

"Brooklyn!" He sounded offended. "Well, at least you said it correctly." She had pronounced it "Nor-Lins.

"We southerners have to stick together." She noticed he was still holding the tray. "Here, let me take that. You can come in for a minute if you like."

"You only have one cup," he pointed out helpfully.

"You can drink from the saucer," Jez said.

"Are you vamping me, Red?"

"Who, I?" she said innocently.

"I'm sorry, I can't go for a woman with good grammar."

She laughed, set the tray on the bureau, and poured a cup of tea. It trailed vapor like a comet. She sipped. "Hmmm. Good." Passed him the cup. "How long did you live in New Orleans?"

"Twelve years." He sipped, handed her the cup.

"Great town. Why'd you leave? Folks move?"

"No." He accepted the cup from her. "Mother died." For a moment, he just held the cup, not drinking, not listening. Not there.

The moment stretched out.

Jez snapped her fingers in front of his face. "Come on back to me, boy."

He blinked. Smiled. "Here I am."

"There you are." She smiled back. "I'm sorry about your mother."

"Long time ago. Her name was Ondine." *Why am I telling her this?*

"The little mermaid." She knew the story.

"Here I am, all cozy with a great-looking redhead, who's practically got me eating out of her hand"—he toasted her with the teacup—"and what do we talk about? My dear, departed mummy. You're going to ruin my reputation."

Boom, crash. It was as if he'd slammed a door shut. A trick mirror she'd been permitted to look through briefly but with no knowledge of what to look for or at. Sigmund Freud, where are you when I need you, she thought.

"Strangers waiting for a bus," he said suddenly.

"Huh?"

"The feeling of intimacy between people who are really little more than strangers," he explained. "The three of us."

"I suppose in the cold light of morning, we'll all be strangers again."

"No, it'll just cool out to normal speed."

That made sense to her somehow. "You're pretty smart for someone so obnoxious."

He shrugged. "I hang around a lot of mental wards."

"I never know when you're kidding."

He smiled, a Mona Lisa, no-you-can't-see-my-teeth smile. "I wish we weren't working together."

"Thanks a lot!"

"Can't get involved with people you work with. Hey . . ." He threw his hands up in a helpless gesture. "You screwed up."

She laughed, escorting him to the door. "I think I'm better off this way."

"Really?"

"Sure. Instead of one guy, I got two."

"Only our hearts," Micah declared dramatically.

"You shall never have our bodies. Unless, of course, you book ahead. And arrange for separate accommodations."

"Right." She continued to push him gently toward the door. "Do you suppose you and I could work out the same sort of deal you and Steve have?"

He looked blank. "You lost me there."

"After the mission," she said softly, amused. "We'll talk about that wrestling match."

"But I don't want to wrestle Steve."

"That's it, get out!" She propelled him out the door.

"Wait a sec," he called from the hallway. "I got this for you." He handed her a small paperback, pulled from a back pocket. A guide to Thailand.

"Thanks." She yawned suddenly. " 'Scuse me."

"Good night, Cookie."

"Good night, hotshot." She watched him go down the hall to his room. Watched him. She didn't hear his footsteps. Well, soft carpeting . . . naw, these guys were good.

Then again, so was Toby Cooke's little girl. She slid between the cool, fresh sheets, feeling her fatigue rush in at her. Too tired to sleep. She got out of bed and flipped on the TV. Debbie Reynolds gabbled fluently in Thai. Jez got the sound down to barely audible and crawled back to bed.

She thought about the two men; mercurial Micah, the original mood-a-minute man, and introspective Steve Sinclair, who made dependability mysterious and enticing. John Garfield and Gary Cooper.

Or the makings of a *super* porn film.

But are you here just to look at the scenery, she asked herself?

To find Tina's murderer, part of her still insisted. But Jez knew better. She wasn't doing this solely for Tina. It was for herself as well.

In some bizarre way, she belonged. To that moment, and to the mission. Running around like a decapitated chicken, she had still stumbled on her destiny.

The woman warrior returning to the native shore. Without shield, without sword. But still . . . home, finally at home.

"Jez, my girl," she murmured sleepily. "Either you're tired, or you're brilliant. And I think you're tired." She turned onto one side and was soon asleep.

chapter 11

" 'Bangkok, nicknamed City of Angels, boasts many impressive and breathtaking pieces of architecture.' " Jez read from her guidebook.

Sinclair wore a pained expression; he'd gotten the tour already, thank you very much, courtesy of the U.S. Army. His tour had been in Nam, but most of Southeast Asia looked the same to him. Great culture, incredible poverty.

"Really," Jez insisted. "This is great stuff. 'The Temple of the Emerald Buddha looms largest, with its gold-encrusted walls and roofs tiled in gleaming green and orange porcelain,' " she read. " 'Giant demons, studded with chips of colored glass and china, hover or lurk in nooks, all over the temple, symbolically offering protection from evil spirits.

" 'The National Assembly Hall, whose silhouette closely resembles the American White House, combines iron parapets and domes with intricate stone carvings. Originally built to house the throne room, it is the current seat of the National Parliament.' "

Jez looked up, disappointed. "Damn, it does look like the White House."

Grinning, Micah swooped down on her, grabbing the book from her hands. He started to read out loud, aping her soft Texas accent. " 'Not far from the Temple of the Emerald Buddha stands the Grand Palace, best known to the world because of *The King and I*.' "

People were starting to stare.

" 'The palace was at one time the home of Anna and the King of Siam, and was built for King Mongut, his thirty-five wives, and eighty-two children.' Busy guy," Micah commented.

He looked across the Grand Palace to the Pramane Ground, now a public park, though once King Mongut's saddling-up area for elephants. Jez absorbed that fact with a certain amount of skepticism. How would you saddle an elephant, anyway?

"Look, kite fighting!" Micah yelled. He flipped Jez's book into the air and dashed off.

Sinclair caught the book and, anticipating Jez's next question, turned to the page that explained kite fighting. "There you go."

"Thanks." She smiled at him. No doubt about it, Sinclair thought. If they weren't working together, that smile would have melted a few of his fillings.

" 'Thai kite fighting,' " she read. " 'The rules are complicated and date back many centuries. It is essentially an aerial dogfight. . . . Spectators gather nightly to watch the huge paper flyers swoop majestically overhead.' "

"Look," Micah whispered in her ear. She jumped a little. It would probably take some time before she adjusted to the fact that he could get around as silently as an Indian.

She sighted along his pointing finger, fascinated by the fluid movement of the kites, which were operated by large teams of strong-armed men. The sight of the colorful missiles circling around the late-afternoon sky was visually dazzling.

Sinclair, while realizing the need to soak up some local color and the desire to unwind after the long flight, mostly wanted to get on with the case.

Micah was trying to explain the finer points of the sport. "The bigger kite is called a *chula*. The smaller, more mobile one, called *pakpao*"—he shot a look toward Jez—"is the female."

Sinclair found himself becoming more interested. "Are those protruberances on the *chula* metal barbs?"

"Mm-hm. More sexual metaphor. The barbs on the *chula* represent the male genitalia, and the big loop in the *pakpao* represents the female."

"And the winner?"

"Is the one who pulls the other down onto the ground in his or her territory."

"And I suppose"—Sinclair tried to illustrate with his hands—"the more aggressive male attacks, relying on his superior size and strength."

Micah nodded several times. "While the weaker, coyer female tries to lure the male into her territory and so gain an advantage."

"Come into my web, said the spider to the fly," Jez purred.

Both men laughed.

"But how," Sinclair asked in an excited voice, "given the male's superior strength and size, does the female ever win?"

Micah and Jez answered in unison. "Leverage."

Sinclair remembered Jez's expertise in the martial arts and felt a little foolish. "Right. Guess I'm more tired than I thought."

As if illustrating the tactic expressly for their benefit, the *pakpao* team, having teased the *chula* team in with a series of quick spiraling movements, was at that moment finishing off its opponent with a graceful angular swoop from above. The *chula* thunked to the ground, held from above by the victorious *pakpao*.

The crowd cheered wildly—Sinclair, Jez, and Micah as enthusiastically as the rest.

"I shot a prick into the air," Micah said.

"Brought down by a pussy, I know not where," Jez responded.

They giggled and gave each other five.

"Can we get down to business now, sports fans?" Sinclair asked.

Micah and Jez shifted their attention instantly to Sinclair. He pulled out a small leather-bound black book. "Since we have never worked as a team before, the Librarian thought it best to outline our M.O. for this assignment very specifically."

"M.O.?" Jez asked meekly, not wanting to appear ignorant.

"Modus operandi," Sinclair answered.

Jez still looked puzzled.

"Plan," Micah said dryly.

"You mean the Librarian plans our strategy from several thousand miles away?"

Sinclair nodded.

"But what if things don't go according to plan?"

"We stay in close contact with the Librarian, and call in periodically for instructions. But we're not robots."

Micah added. "We weren't chosen for this mission casually. One of the Librarian's basic criteria for agents is the ability to think and react quickly and independently. I've never known him to make a mistake. We're the team for the job."

Jez appreciated the vote of confidence, especially coming from the man who only yesterday had wanted to send her packing. She threw up her hands. "All right," she said, turning to Sinclair, "what's our M.O. for tomorrow?"

Sinclair laughed and consulted his book. "Dreamscape Films is holding auditions for young actresses tomorrow."

"But I've never done any acting."

"Had Tina, before she came to Thailand?"

"You mean, I'll be auditioning to replace my sister?"

"The newspaper ad doesn't say so, but I think we can safely assume that. Remember, they were in the middle of filming when Tina was killed. They'll want to save the expense of shooting all that footage over again by hiring someone who closely resembles her."

"Won't they be suspicious of the resemblance?"

Sinclair shook his head. "There'll be a lot of redheads there. Girls with dyed hair, high-heeled shoes, and light-colored makeup, all trying to look as much like Tina as possible. But you'll be the closest match."

"And if that's not enough?"

Sinclair directed the point of his felt-tipped pen at Micah. "We always keep an ace in the hole."

Jez extended her long legs, crossing them at the ankle, and nodded slowly. "And what will you be doing?"

"Visiting an old . . ." Sinclair searched for the

right word, finally settling on "partner." Jez and Micah exchanged a look of surprise. "Marty Phillips, our contact here. Marty's supposed to tell me how Dreamscape Films could be transporting such large quantities of snow so efficiently."

Jez smiled. "Their M.O."

"Right." Sinclair got up. Jez and Micah followed suit. "Let's head back to the hotel." They left the Pramane Ground, as the two kite-fighting teams were trying to disengage the *chula* and the *pakpao*. A final, concerted tug succeeded in separating the two kites, but it was executed with such force that each splintered into a litter of useless fragments.

chapter 12

"Hiya."

Jez craned her neck around in the cramped elevator to see who was talking to her. She gaped; if there'd been room, she would have taken a step back in amazement.

"Hi," she said finally. The girl who'd spoken to her was oriental, not unlike the women Jez had seen that morning from her hotel-room window bicycling to work; a little younger, a little prettier, but very much the same. Spoiling her Asian delicacy was the incredible shock of bright red hair she sported.

"You here for the audition?" the Chinese girl asked.

"Uh, yes."

She gave Jez an appraising look. "Just my luck." She ran her fingers through her carroty mop. It was tacky with spray and it took her a moment to disengage her hand. "They're probably going to type out all the oriental girls first, anyway."

Jez didn't understand what the girl meant, so she kept quiet.

"Nancy Dallas," the Chinese girl introduced herself. "Real American name, huh?"

"Real American," Jez agreed, shaking the hand offered to her. "I'm ..." she had to think for a moment. "Sheri Nolan." Suposedly, the Librarian had issued her that alias, but Jez thought she detected Micah's fine hand in there somewhere.

"Nice name," Nancy said. The elevator doors slid open, admitted more redheads, and then slammed shut with a hydraulic hiss. One more floor. "You make it up, or did your agent?"

"My agent," Jez answered promptly. Boy, if you only knew what kind of agent; Jez smirked. If she wasn't scared half out of her mind, she would have been laughing hysterically. Nancy Dallas really cracked her up.

The elevator door opened, and Jez, Nancy, and the rest of the redheaded league joined the auburn swarm milling around in the corridor.

Jez noticed that Nancy was walking strangely. At first she thought the girl was hurt. On second thought she realized she'd been right the first time: walking on four-inch heels was enough to give anybody considerable pain. Nancy's walk was further impaired by the tight skirt stretched across her rump. The result was the walk that made Marilyn Monroe immortal. Apparently, Nancy had graduated from the college of old movies as well as the school of hard knocks.

It was a vain attempt. Jez still towered over the oriental girl, and Tina had had a few inches on Jez. Most of the other women were attempting the same masquerade, trying to exchange their own natural oriental beauty for a ludicrous copy of Tina's Anglo charm.

Every shade of red hair was represented, from strawberry blond to a pinky purple Jez had only seen in New York's Greenwich Village. Everywhere women lurched in their high-rise heels. Jez felt like a confident gazelle in her pretty low-heeled sandals. She wore a simple cotton dress in her favorite turquoise. Its oriental design only enhanced her foreignness. An elephant among field mice but a beautiful one.

Actually, she didn't feel like an elephant, or a gazelle; she felt like the fatted calf. Both Sinclair and Micah had helped her "prepare" for this audition; they'd even had a little argument over her choice of dress. (Micah had preferred hot pink.)

After she was all dressed and ready to go, Micah had given her eye drops. They made her eyes sparkly and luminous: intelligent sapphires. Jez was ready to run out and buy a quart of the stuff when she thought to ask what it was.

Micah looked uncomfortable. "Belladonna."

"Belladonna? You mean the narcotic?"

"Uh-huh." That was from Sinclair, at the other end of the hotel room, reading the Koran—Micah's witticism for the Thai version of *TV Guide*.

Jez had said in a tiny voice, "Isn't that illegal?"

Both men threw their hands in the air in disgust. She understood. This beauty contest was no beauty contest. She had to get that part, even if it meant stacking the deck.

She looked in the mirror. She'd never looked more beautiful in her life.

The actresses were herded into a large reception area, past a door that read PRIVATE. ABSOLUTELY NO UNAUTHORIZED PERSONEL. Guess they don't mean us, Jez thought.

There weren't enough seats inside; a lot of women remained standing, some still out in the hallway. Nancy squeezed onto the couch next to Jez. Without her heels she probably lied about making five feet.

Behind the desk was an attractive Thai woman, around Jez's age, maybe a little older. It was hard to tell. She wore an off-white raw-silk pants suit with a mustard blouse, open just enough to see the tops of her high breasts. Her black hair was lustrous and full.

She looked very familiar to Jez.

The Thai woman got up from the desk, holding a clipboard. Her smile was the practiced display of teeth a model learns to wear like armor.

"She thinks she's so hot," Nancy was saying. "That beauty contest was six years ago and she was only runner-up."

"First runner-up," another girl put in. "Her name's Barbara Tiang."

Jez grinned; she happened to have been watching that beauty contest. Miss Tiang's smile had faded somewhat as the winner was being crowned. Jez couldn't fault her for being human.

"Thank you all for coming here," Barbara said. "Before we take your pictures and resumes, we're going to type out so we don't waste your time. Okay?"

Nobody said it wasn't. Under Miss Tiang's direction, the first twenty girls lined up single file. Nancy was chattering to Jez about something or the other, so she didn't see the two men enter the reception area.

They both provoked strong if opposing reactions from Jez. One man, a slim Thai in his early thirties, wore a University of Chicago sweat shirt and black cotton trousers. Jez assumed that he would be the partner in any martial-arts demonstrations that might be required for the audition. She was glad it wasn't the other man. Very glad.

Barbara Tiang and the two men swept down the row of actresses. The man Jez didn't like led the parade, followed by Chicago East, with Barbara bringing up the rear.

As the first man approached, each woman who fell under his scrutiny shied away, either moving her feet restlessly or just gazing at the ground. Even tough little Nancy couldn't hold her ground.

Jez managed by keeping her eyes fastened on the Thai man. As he walked by, Jez called out, "Hello, Chicago."

He looked a little startled but recovered. "Hello, Red." He grinned back.

Obviously she'd made an impression. Score one for our side, Jez thought. The first man seemed to be giving signals to Barbara. At any rate she was scribbling away like a madwoman.

The trio marched back to the head of the line.

"Okay," Barbara said cheerfully. "Would the girl in the black skirt"—that was Nancy—"and the girl in the blue dress"—Jez let out the breath she'd been holding for a year—"please stay. The rest of you, thank you very much." She walked over to the door. "Will the next group of twenty please come in?"

In the hall, there were sounds of combat. Somebody not in the top twenty was expressing her resentment.

Nancy gave Jez a hug. "We made it, Sheri!"

Who's Sheri? Jez thought blearily. She was going to have to start wearing a name tag.

Barbara was approaching them, her smile fixed firmly in place. "Ladies, we have a dressing room for you to change into your swimsuits." Her model's smile slipped, replaced by one of her genuine humor. "Guess I've heard that phrase a few times. Swimsuit competition, next."

Nancy grabbed Jez's arm. "Okey-dokey, come on, Sheri."

The dressing room was pretty posh; it reminded Jez of Beautiful Universe. Dreamscape may not be legit but it definitely seemed solvent. She and Nancy chose lockers and started peeling.

They were joined by two ther women, a tall blond with a German accent and a beautiful Chinese-American model with a deep auburn mane.

Looking at Jez's hair, she held out a strand of her own. "Clairol." She shrugged philosophically. "You?"

"Uhhh, nature's bounty, I'm afraid." Jez shucked off her bra and panties, stepping into her bikini bottom.

"That ain't all that's real," Nancy put in, staring at Jez's chest.

Hurriedly, Jez put on the bra top of her bikini. It didn't hide more than it had to. She would have loved to trade it for Nancy's white one-piece job. The Chinese girl had demurely turned her back to don it.

Jez had a slim gold chain around her midriff; its clasp tickled her bare belly. The clasp held a small signaling device. Just in case Plan B was called for.

The blond was quiet. Jez was puzzled as to why

she hadn't dyed her hair. Probably just a ploy to get attention. (Like yelling "Hi, Chicago.") Her name was Toni and she was a stewardess. For the Red Baron, Jez bet. She was also a bitch.

The Chinese-American model was actually a Chinese-English actress named Jillian. She had studied drama in London, and done Shakespeare there. She'd come to Thailand with a touring theater company, lost her money somehow, and been stranded. An audition seemed like as good a time waster as starving.

Nancy herself said she'd been chosen to appease the Thai actor's union.

"I wish us all luck," Jillian said in her soft voice.

Toni laughed. "I don't. We can be honest, yes?" She went over to the full-length mirror, admiring herself.

"We can," Nancy said. "You can be a cunt, Brunhilde."

Before they could tangle further, Barbara entered. "Everybody changed?"

They all nodded, which was dumb, obviously they had changed. They followed Barbara back into the reception area and sat on the couch as she directed them. Jez felt her bare thighs sticking to the couch.

"Who would have a leather couch in Thailand?" Jillian complained.

"Ladies, I would like to introduce"—Barbara was pointing to the man Jez hadn't liked—"Lieutenant Juan Valjenos"—*a creep and a lech*—"and"—now she indicated Chicago East—"Tim Chang."

Valjenos nodded grandly. Chang settled for a cheery "Hi, kids." Jez assumed the "let's put on a show" was understood.

She studied Valjenos as Barbara continued her welcome-to-the-semifinals speech. The "lieutenant" sat oddly on him. He seemed more militarylike than military. In Jez's neck of the woods, they would have said he was trying too hard.

"Bet he's enjoying the tits-and-ass parade." Nancy said.

"Miss Nolan?"

Jez bolted to her feet, praying her little green bikini decided to go along for the ride.

Tim Chang handed her a sheet of paper. "Relax." He smiled at her. "You'll be fine."

She read the lines on the paper.

"Out loud, please."

Jez sighed. "We know all about your scheme, Mr. Shinato. People aren't going to stand for this much longer. Your first and last mistake was taking on the Circle of Eight." She had no idea what the hell she was saying. Barbara and Tim looked equally perplexed. Jez had a feeling she had crapped out on the reading.

Nancy went next, shrieking the lines at the top of her voice. Toni's accent seemed a problem, and then it was Jillian's turn at bat.

Her trained voice gave life to the lines Jez, Nancy, and Toni had butchered. Oh, that's how you do it, Jez thought.

Tim looked at Jillian meltingly. Valjenos seemed less impressed.

The next obstacle course was a brief fight, choreographed by Tim Chang. He explained the moves in simple terms.

A few simple blocks checking his forehand slash, a kick to the midsection on the right side, twisting to a hip roll. All she had to do was remember everything.

Toni was a composition of studied cool. She went through the exercise with competence and skill, barely breaking into a sweat. At its completion, she threw Valjenos a stiff salute.

He bowed with mock formality. "I've always admired Germanic efficiency." The mouth smiled; the eyes kept their distance.

Jillian was called next.

"I'm afraid the jig is up." She smiled apologetically. "I'm not a fighter. I'd hoped my reading might be good enough to persuade you . . ." Tim looked crestfallen. ". . . obviously not. Sorry for wasting your time."

She whirled, heading for the locker room.

Tim caught up with her. "Uh, could you hang around, anyway? I really enjoyed your reading."

Jillian gave him a blinding smile. "I'd love to, Tim."

This time Tim Chang did not melt . . . he evaporated.

Jillian sat down next to Nancy, smiling at her feet.

"Bet I know where your next meal's coming from." Nancy chortled. Then she was on her feet, answering Barbara's page.

"I got it." She nodded briskly, taking a rather bizarre stance. Jez doubted she'd been schooled anyplace other than the Bangkok slums.

Tim made his opening move. Nancy grabbed him, one hand at his neck, the other at his crotch, threw him, and charged in, aiming for his groin.

"Arghhh!" Tim covered up inelegantly, lying on his back, legs waving in the air, both hands trying to protect the family jewels. Valjenos snickered; Barbara just looked bored. Then Tim remembered Jillian was there and made a nice effort to recover his dignity.

"I don't go for no fancy Dan moves," Nancy explained calmly.

Valjenos crooked his finger at her; she approached him warily.

His eyes crawled over her: perky breasts, little belly, rounded knees. "How badly do you want this part?"

Nancy's body blocked Jez's view of Valjenos, but Jez had a horrible feeling he had unzipped his fly. That was impossible. Maybe he was just going to ask her to take back some overdue library books.

Nancy sidled away. "Mister, I don't need no job that bad." She walked past Jez. "Well, I'm out. I just gotta hang around to see you beat out the Teutonic Tit." She smiled acidly at Toni as she moved over to the garbage bin by Barbara's desk.

"Now that it's all over . . ." she announced wickedly. In a second, she had pulled off and discarded the red wig, letting her jet mane cascade down to her waist. Arching her back, she dipped both hands down the front of her swimsuit and pulled out two monstrous falsies. They joined the wig in the trash. The swimsuit shrunk back against her now-girlish body.

Jez grinned. The Mystery of the Shy Chinagirl, solved at last.

It was her turn. She listened carefully to Tim's instructions, nodding every time he looked at her for acknowledgment. She was completely lost.

To make matters worse, fighting while wearing a bikini was not Jez's idea of simplicity. She couldn't remember whether she was supposed to fake left or right before she chopped. She decided left.

It was the wrong choice. Like a gentle tiger, Tim had her pinned and doing her impression of an upended turtle.

Always a favorite at parties, Jez thought wildly. Upside down she read Valjenos's expression—disappointment.

Time for Plan B.

Jez touched her navel chain, depressing the clasp. Precisely fifteen seconds later, the door was flung open and a tea cart was pushed in, followed by the vendor, a rough-looking man of about fifty, his white paper hat awry. He seemed a little drunk.

"Tea?" he called out. "Tea? Rice cakes? Very good."

"We don't want any tea," Barbara said.

Jez was biting her lip to keep from laughing. Micah's disguise was pretty darn good, though to her it was transparent.

He'd given up trying to sell tea and rice cakes.

"Fucky-fuck, nice ladies?" he said, still smiling. "French, round-the-world?" He reached for Jez's bikini top, locking eyes with her.

NOW.

She grabbed him by both shoulders, yanking him up as she slid off the couch. Micah thudded into the wall, chunking out plaster with his boots. Girls fled.

Out of the corner of her eye, Jez saw Tim rise to assist her and Valjenos hold him back. Score two more points for Gentleman Tim, minus one for a-creep-and-a-lech.

Micah grabbed her, both hands around her waist.

She kicked up, flipping over his body, smacking both knees into his shoulder blades on her descent. He grabbed both her feet, spilling her onto the floor. She clamped both ankles in a binding pinch just above his hipbones and dumped him on his head.

"Sissy," Micah panted in a whisper. In answer, she aimed a chop for his neck. He blocked and slammed a kick at her back, powerless but deadly looking.

Jez took the fall and retreated to Barbara's desk, perching on top. Barbara had long since vacated. When the wild tea-cart man leaped at her, legs poised for a killer kick, she just hopped off and let him crash into the desk. It didn't break.

Jez threw him in the chair with enough force to send it careening into the wall. The chair broke.

"All right!" Nancy squealed.

Micah got up groggily, took one look at an advancing Jez, and screamed. "She is a devil!" He made the sign of the evil eye. "A she-tiger in a woman's body!" He sidled past her to the door and hit the hall running.

Jez gave chase, whooping like an Indian. Somehow she knew Valjenos was still watching; the show might be over, he was waiting for a curtain call.

As an encore, she booted Micah into a conveniently empty elevator. He fairly flew in, landing in a heap in the far corner and lying there with closed eyes.

I hope I haven't killed him, Jez thought. She leaned over him; at this angle no one in the hall could see them.

"Are you all right?" she whispered.

He leaned up and kissed her quickly, grinning. "You're beautiful when you're angry."

"Oh, you," Jez said helplessly, letting the elevator door close.

The hallway was empty. Jez padded back to the reception area. The goddamn tea cart was still sitting there.

Calming her shaking hands, Jez poured a cup. She looked over at Valjenos. "Cream or lemon?"

"Barbara, prepare a contract for Miss Nolan," Valjenos ordered. He took the cup from Jez and dumped it in the garbage. "I don't care for tea, Miss Nolan. My tastes are somewhat more sophisticated."

The other girls were leaving. For a brief second Jez realized that this had been a good part of Tina's life: meeting people, getting to like them, and then never seeing them again. Maybe there was a side to Tina she didn't know about, a strength she'd never known Tina had.

Good-byes were in progress. Tim was getting Jillian's phone number; Nancy tossed off a casual "Eat shit, Heidi" as an affectionate farewell to Toni.

"Nancy," Jez called out, "I'm sorry you didn't get the part."

Nancy smiled. *"Mai penrai."*

"What?"

"Never mind."

"Sorry."

"No." Nancy giggled. "That's what it means, never mind."

Jez looked relieved. She then remembered what her dad used to say to Tina. "See you in the movies."

Nancy gave her a thumbs-up. "You bet. See you."
Jez hoped so.

Barbara swept over and gave Jez a big hug.

"I'm so glad you got the part." She stepped back, looking intently into the redhead's face. "Pretty eyes," she mused. "Are you a user?" Before Jez could answer she went on. "It doesn't matter, not to me." She embraced Jez again, holding her body very close.

A very hot lady, this Barbara Tiang. Jez shifted away, uncomfortable.

Barbara smiled. "Welcome to Dreamscape."

chapter 13

Sinclair sat up in bed groggily and rubbed his eyes.

The clock on the nightstand read 11:15. Aw, shit, he thought. Fucking jet lag will do it to you every time.

He lifted the receiver on the dialless hotel telephone. An operator answered almost immediately. "Main desk. May I help you?"

"Yes, this is Mr. Henegan in Room 1601. Could you send up a pot of something hot with caffeine in it?"

"Right away, Mr. Henegan."

"Thanks."

"Oh, and Mr. Henegan?"

"Yes?"

"You have a message."

"Oh?"

"From your friend Mr. Simmons in 1603."

Sinclair closed his eyes. "Read it to me please."

"It says, 'Dear Pop, Gone to the movies with Sis. Thought you needed the sleep. Be back by four.' And it's signed 'M'. Does that sound right to you?''

Sinclair managed a weak smile. Cocky little bastard, he thought. "Absolutely. Thank you, operator."

"You're welcome. I'll send a pot of tea right up."

"I appreciate it," he said, and hung up.

Sinclair rolled out of bed. He consulted the clock again. Better skip the morning workout, he thought, and headed straight for the bathroom.

A bracing shower was just what he needed, though he could never manage to get the water in these hotel showers quite as hot as he liked. Still, it fell invigoratingly over his thick-muscled shoulders, washboard stomach, and rock-hard thighs. He toweled and off and shaved quickly.

When he emerged from the steamy bathroom, a pot of fragrant tea was sitting on the dresser.

Sinclair poured a cup, its aromatic vapor invading his nostrils, and downed it in one swallow. It was very hot, just the way he liked it. He immediately poured another, and taking it in one hand and the handle of his back attaché case in the other, he settled back on the bed.

He pulled from the attaché case a device which resembled a hockey puck, except that it was equipped with several numbered buttons. He grabbed the phone from the nightstand and, using the case as a table, placed the device, his cup of tea, and the phone on it.

He lifted the receiver and unscrewed the mouthpiece, replacing it with the pucklike device. He punched four buttons to identify himself as Agent Steven Sinclair, then four more to place his call. There was a second or two of static followed by the voice of the Librarian.

"Steve?"

"Yes, sir?"

"The gulf winds have recently turned colder."

"Uh." Sinclair closed his eyes tightly, tried to remember the answering phrase. "Something about pink salmon rushing upstream. Look, I said it was me, didn't I?"

"So you did." The Librarian tried not to sound too disappointed. "Are your new associates working out satisfactorily?"

"It's a little early to tell, isn't it?"

"Given your natural pessimism, I'll take that as an affirmative response. Have you gotten in touch with Marty Phillips yet?"

"No."

"Why not?" the Librarian asked, testily.

"Sir, I don't mean to doubt your judgment." Sinclair paused, searching his brain for the right words; how not to offend this man he respected above all others. Seconds dragged by. Finally he spoke, tentatively. "I will get in touch with Marty when I think the time is right." He tried to tread carefully. "I don't think I need as tight a rein as some of the less experienced agents."

"I'm sure you know best," the Librarian instantly countered. His icy tone carried a different message. "After you have made contact, get back to me." The line went dead.

Sinclair cursed vehemently and repeatedly as he replaced the mouthpiece, dressed, and hit the crowded Bangkok's streets.

He took a *samlor*—Bangkok's three-wheeled taxi—to Chinatown, the city's seamiest district, the scene of Tina Cooke's murder.

It was a hot, humid day. The stink of garbage

rose from the steaming pavement to assault him when he emerged from the *samlor*. Derelicts, junkies, and prostitutes lined the dirty streets. Picturesque, he thought. I guess every city has one.

He put on his wire-rimmed sunglasses and started walking.

"He-ey, baby, want a date?" sang a heavily accented low voice. Sinclair turned to see a tall hooker beckoning to him from a doorway. She had red hair. Sinclair thought immediately of Jez, hoped everything was going according to plan at Dreamscape Films.

The hooker ran her tongue around the outline of her lips and rocked her head slowly from side to side, moaning, "C'mon, baby, show you a good time. C'mon, baby."

She extended her arms toward him, and Sinclair saw the long vertical tracks that indicated a mainliner. She *was* what he was looking for.

He approached her. "What's your name?"

She laughed gutturally, rested her hands lightly on his shoulders. "Nicole."

"Nicole," Sinclair whispered, running an index finger gently along the tracks on her left arm, "where can I get happy?"

"Aw," Nicole purred, pressing her forehead against his, "what you want that for when you got me? What you want that for when you got me?"

Sinclair, who had three twenty-baht bills concealed in his palm, flashed them briefly in front of Nicole's eyes, then tucked them into her ample cleavage. "I have this problem," he whispered. "Social disease."

She backed away from him, her whole body shaking with laughter. "I don't believe you, cutie."

She looked down at the bills nestled between her breasts. "But you nice. Ramkamheng. Two blocks down, one block over." She stuck the end of her thumb in her mouth and nodded a few times. "Ramkamheng."

"Thank you, Nicole." He kissed her lightly on the forehead and started off down the street.

"Come back if you get better," Nicole shouted after him, then collapsed, laughing, in the doorway.

Ramkamheng was a bar, named after a Thai warrior-king from the thirteenth century. Captioned pictures adorned the walls, chronicling the life of the legendary monarch.

The name and the pictures were the only majestic things about the bar. It smelled almost as bad as the street outside. The patrons vied for space with the insects.

Sinclair took off his sunglasses as he entered the dingy saloon and stuffed them in his shirt pocket. A few haggard men were slumped over the bar. There was a pool table in one corner, illuminated by a single light bulb, dangling from the ceiling. Sinclair smiled and shook his head, knowing he could be in any of a hundred cities; the dives all came out of the same cookie cutter.

He sat on the nearest bar stool, close to a light, and ordered a glass of the local beer.

It wasn't long before he felt a firm insistent tapping on the shoulder. "Hey, white meat, you wander too far from the tour bus?" Laughter.

At least three, maybe more, Sinclair calculated. He paid for his beer and took a swallow. It was slightly sour, but quenching.

He set his glass back down on the bar. The tapping returned, harder than before.

"Hey, maybe you don't hear so good, chalky. This is strictly yellow bar. No Westerners allowed."

Sinclair raised his glass as if to drink and, aiming for the owner of the voice, threw the contents over his shoulder.

Ourtaged curses answered.

Before they had a chance to react, he spun around on the bar stool and pummeled the nearest thug repeatedly in the stomach. Grunts of pain followed the steady thuds made by Sinclair's powerful fists hitting the soft belly of his potential attacker. When the man began to crumple, Sinclair sailed a hard right through his jaw that sent him and several teeth flying. He landed in a heap near the jukebox, and didn't think once about getting up.

Another one, short and wide, backed up a few paces and charged, head-first. This is just too easy, Sinclair thought. He waited until the man was almost upon him, then stepped coolly aside. The head barreled into the sturdy bar and followed the body to the floor. After a few shakes, its owner somehow rose to his feet, still bent over at the waist. Sinclair locked his hands together and, raising them high over his head, brought them crashing down on the back of the thick neck. This time it stayed where it was.

Breathing heavily and feeling more charged up than he could remember feeling in years, Sinclair turned to face the rest of the attack squad.

There were two. Neither looked anxious to pick up where his pals had left off. One was tall and weasellike and attached to a pool cue. The other was short and weasellike and held out in front of him a slender object which could have been a switchblade or which could have been a comb. They spent at least a minute looking from Sinclair to each other to Sinclair to each other, as if expecting or hoping the other would go for Sinclair and leave plenty of running room.

Seeing their dilemma, Sinclair, much as he wanted to beat the shit out of them, decided to do the gentlemanly thing. He raised his hands in a peacemaking gesture. "Okay, boys, let's call it a draw," he said.

The little weasel seemed eager to comply. He exhaled with relief and, unzipping the pocket of his leather jacket, put away the still-unidentified slender object.

The big weasel, however, reacted in a totally unexpected way. As if suddenly fortified by an invisible force, he stood up straight and widened his stance, challenging. His face took on a fierce, menacing expression.

At first, Sinclair thought it was a joke. But not when he saw the big weasel take hold of the pool cue with both hands like a baseball bat and swing it back above his shoulders like Reggie Jackson preparing to hit a home run.

Sinclair ducked in time and the cue stick whizzed over his head. It hit the little weasel squarely in the mouth. His eyes became as big as saucers, he screamed, blood gushed from his mouth in a torrent, and his hands reached up to staunch the flow, all in a matter of seconds.

Sinclair didn't need a second invitation. He took hold of the cue stick with both hands. The big weasel changed his grip slightly, and held on for dear life, a bulldog tenaciously grasping his only bone.

For a split second it looked like a tug-o-war. But Sinclair didn't feel like playing anymore. Concentrating his strength at a point near the center of his body, he thrust powerfully up and forward. The big weasel's body expanded like an umbrella and flew backward in a wide arc, as if self-propelled. It landed faceup on the pool table, right ear in the side pocket.

The little weasel was leaning on the bar, crying, his hands still covering his bleeding mouth. Sinclair ordered him a beer, stuck it under his nose. "Wash your mouth out with this."

The little weasel took it.

"Who's the leader?"

The little weasel pointed limply at the one near the jukebox; Sinclair's first victim.

"What's his name?"

"Mri-ee."

Sinclair turned to the bartender. "What's he saying?"

"Richie."

"Oh. Richie." Sinclair grinned broadly at the little weasel.

He ordered another beer and carried it over to Richie's hammock. Three gentle foot nudges had no effect. So Sinclair poured the contents of the beer glass over his head, and Richie came instantly, splutteringly, awake. He thought he was having a bad dream until he opened his eyes and saw the big American looming over him.

"Now, Richie," Sinclair said in a controlled but threatening voice, "it happens I'm throwing a little party tonight. A friend of mine tells me you're the man to see about refreshments."

"Uh, sure man. What kinda shit you looking for?"

"Snow."

"Aw, geez. I'm cold, man. Christmas is late this month."

"Well, when can I get some?"

"Soon. Soon. It shoulda come in yesterday. Look, you give me your address and when it comes in I personally—"

Sinclair grabbed him by the lapels. "You better be telling me the truth."

"I am, man, I am, I swear." His voice was fast and excited.

Sinclair lifted him to his feet and shoved him against the jukebox. "Because if you're not I . . ." he stopped abruptly, and let go of Richie's jacket. For the first time, Sinclair could see his face, the light from the jukebox illuminating it.

"Where'd you get that mark?"

"What mark, man?"

"On your cheek."

"Oh, that. That's my certification," Richie said proudly. "My big boss, he give it to me. Never seen nothing like it before, have you?"

"No," Sinclair lied. Only in the photographs of Tina Cooke's corpse, he thought. And on Amanda.

"Yeah, see how it looks a little bit like the face of a snake? My big boss, he has this ring, see, looks just like a snake, and the top of it is the snake's head. It's his trademark, kinda. He rubs the ring in this little jar he always carries, then he gives you the mark. It hurts a lot," he boasted.

"I'll bet," Sinclair said in a flat voice. He backed away from Richie a few paces, needing the distance.

He tried to keep his mind focused on the job at hand, but it was hard when all he could think about was Amanda.

"Hey man, something the matter?" Richie asked, sensing a possible chance to run.

"No." Sinclair snapped back to the present and closed in again on the punk. "I'll be back tomorrow, Richie. If you lied to me . . ."

"Hey man! Why would I lie to you? I know you'd bust my face."

Sinclair held him by the lapels again for a long minute, staring hard into his eyes to make sure he was telling the truth before releasing him.

On his way out the door, Sinclair peeled a few bills off his wad and laid them on the bar, telling the bartender, "For your trouble."

The man, who reminded Sinclair vaguely of Ma, nodded soberly.

"And give the quartet a round on me."

The corners of the bartender's mouth turned up a hairsbreadth in an almost-smile. Sinclair responded in kind.

He walked out of the dingy bar into the burning sunlight, satisfied that he had gotten what he came for. He donned his sunglasses and headed back to the hotel.

It was 4:30 when Sinclair finally inserted the key into the lock of his hotel-room door. He'd walked all the way back from the Ramkambeng Bar, hoping to shake the disturbing memories that Richie's scar had triggered.

When he opened the door, a familiar, unpleasant smell greeted him. Durian. Not since Nam had he been treated to what the dictionary called the "strong civet (i.e., catshit) odor" of the durian fruit.

Grown in Thailand, the hard-shelled durian is considered a great delicacy, its creamy pulp prized highly all over Southeast Asia. The GIs, when they could successfully disguise the smell, smuggled large quantities of durian into Nam to use as currency.

Micah was standing on Sinclair's bed, juggling four of the prickly green fruit. Jez was sprawled, spiderlike, in a chair nearby, a tall glass of mineral water in her hand.

At the sight of Sinclair, Micah stopped juggling and let the durian plop onto the bed. "Hey, there he is. How'd it go today with Marty?"

A simple course of action crossed Sinclair's mind, but he knew that he was too tired to kill Micah. He thought of his morning conversation with the Librarian and looked up at Micah standing on his bed. The durian lay like turds underneath him. Sinclair burst out laughing. "I didn't see Marty today, hotshot. And get that catshit fruit off my bed."

"Next question," Jez said.

"How'd your audition go?" Sinclair asked, emptying the contents of his pockets onto the dresser.

Jez raised her glass in a toast. "I got the job. But not without"—she waved her glass in Micah's direction—"a little help from my friend."

Micah was frowning, but his voice was as light as he could make it when he asked Sinclair, "What did you do today?"

"I went to Chinatown." Jez opened her mouth as

if to speak, then took a swallow of her drink instead. "And learned two important pieces of information."

Now that he had hooked them Sinclair decided to wait a minute before reeling them in. He walked deliberately to the bathroom and began to wash his hands.

Neither Micah nor Jez wanted to be the one to break down and ask. For a minute the only sound in the hotel room was that of running water from the bathroom faucets.

Micah looked at Jez, who pointed a long finger at the cluster of durian that still rested at his feet. Taking aim, Micah lobbed one of the fruits in Sinclair's direction. It sailed past his face and landed in the toilet, splashing up water like a pebble in a pond. "Stink bomb," Micah whispered to Jez.

Sinclair groaned, smirked, and turned off the faucets. "One: it's definitely D'Arbanville that we're after. Two: he's in possession of a very large quantity of cocaine—now."

Jez set her glass down. "Meaning?"

"Meaning"—Micah picked up the durian and started juggling again—"if we can crack this soon, before D'Arbanville has a chance to distribute, we can nail his operation red-handed." He tossed the durian one by one out the window. "Tomorrow I've got an interview with Barbara Tiang, Vlajenos's girl Friday. Former Miss Thailand, now script girl and continuity, whatever that means. Bottom line is, she looks to be the eyes and ears of the studio. And highly suggestible."

Jez raised an eyebrow. "Watch yourself in the clinches, Micah, Miss Tiang is a carnivore."

Micah laughed. "So am I, Cookie."

Sinclair turned to Jez before she could retaliate. "Tomorrow," she said, "first day on the set."

"Tomorrow," Sinclair said, "guess I'll talk to Marty." He flushed the last durian away.

chapter 14

Jez couldn't believe that anything that appeared as glamorous as making a movie was really this boring. They'd be breaking for lunch soon and she'd been on the set since six o'clock that morning.

In all that time, she'd had her makeup and hair done. Gold powder was brushed through her hair to pick up the light. The hairdresser cheerfully informed her that it was a bitch to get out and caused horrendous dandruff.

Then she'd been sent to wardrobe. With a morbid thrill, Jez realized she was being outfitted in her dead sister's clothing.

The rest of the morning was spent doing "inserts." Although Tim kindly explained exactly what that meant, all that Jez really understood was that these shots would be edited in to complete some unfinished scenes of Tina's. So she leaped at the camera countless times, always keeping her face carefully averted. The new scenes with "Sheri" would probably be shot in shadowy lighting. The finished product might be dubbed anyway, so Jez's abilities as an actress wouldn't be overtaxed. Then they'd gone through the same process of "inserts" with a heavy-set oriental actor.

He, too, kept his face at a concealing angle.

"Who's he replacing?" Jez had asked Tim as they watched the sweating actor pounce at the camera.

"Sammy Wuan."

Jez reacted. What had Tina written about Sammy Wuan?

No more Sammy . . .

"What happened to him?"

Tim grimaced. "He was a real loner type. Guess he just decided to pack his bags and move on."

"Before the movie was done?"

"Look, Sheri." Tim sighed. "Sammy Wuan was no good and he lost this production quite a lot of money. People around here really don't like to talk about him. Maybe you shouldn't ask around. You know?"

"Sure, Tim," she said easily. Although I would like to ask you, she added silently, why, as you offer me this brotherly advice, you're keeping both eyes glued to Lt. Juan Valjenos.

Why was Tim Chang scared?

Jez remembered what Sinclair had told her: keep her eyes open and her mouth closed. In other words, cool out, Sheri.

"Hey, Tim." She nudged him slyly. "Did you give Jillian a call yet?"

He blushed. Nodded. Blushed a little more. Then proceeded to tell Jez his real ambition: to bring Thai history in theatrical form to Broadway.

Now it was Jez's turn to study Valjenos. Barbara Tiang was talking to him. No, Barbara Tiang was listening to him. Correction, Barbara Tiang was getting instructions from him.

She smiled and pressed a little closer to Valjenos. With a little grin, Valjenos pushed her away carelessly. Rejecting her seemed to give him a lot of pleasure.

Familiarity breeds comtempt, Jez reasoned. He'd probably had Barbara more times than he cared to remember.

He sauntered, if a wooden soldier could be said to saunter, over to Jez.

"Miss Nolan." Without pretense, he stared directly at her breasts.

If my nipples salute him, Jez thought, I'm getting out of here. To hell with the mission.

But he walked past her, not waiting for her reply. It took all her willpower not to turn and watch him go; she knew he was now staring at her ass. Red-hot anger was slowly seeping through her fear. Not yet, though, caution had to be her watchword. Soon enough she'd get her shot at revenge.

She had no proof, no reason; yet she knew this man was Tina's murderer. That Sammy guy, jerk that he was, had probably witnessed the whole thing. He had disappeared all right, the way Jimmy Hoffa had. The way anybody would. Anybody who got in their way.

A hand clamped onto her shoulder. Jez shrieked. Could Valjenos somehow have known what she'd been thinking?

"You're so tense," Barbara murmured, rubbing her shoulders. "The camera picks that right up."

Valjenos must have sent her over. Jez only hoped he hadn't instructed Barbara to stick her tongue in Jez's ear.

It seemed not. Barbara was contentedly massaging her shoulders and neck; doing a good job, too. In spite of herself, Jez felt her muscles relaxing.

"God, that's good," Jez purred. Her eyelids drooped comfortably.

Barbara smiled. "And you thought all I did around here was continuity."

Jez had since learned what continuity meant: remembering from shot to shot whether windows had been opened or closed in the previous scenes, or how an actor had buttoned his shirt that day. All this artifice to convince the audience that what they were seeing was authentic.

Jez didn't think she'd ever enjoy a movie again. Particularly James Bond films. She didn't care if she never saw another one of those as long as she lived.

"You don't think I'm a very nice lady," Barbara said regretfully.

"This business is very tough on women," Jez said. "Anything you have to do to get ahead is okay with me." She grinned. "Doesn't mean I'm not curious, though."

Barbara gobbled the bait. She pointed to one of the cameramen. "See him?"

Jez nodded.

"Likes to be tied up. And that guy"—again she pointed—"he has a thing for high heels. On *his* feet, not mine. And the guy in the green shirt . . ."

I'd better interrupt before she sells the movie rights, Jez thought. "What about Tim?"

"Him?" she said scornfully. "He's scared I'd eat him up alive." She giggled as if the thought appealed to her. "He's the only person here I haven't had."

Jez noticed she hadn't said "man."

"My choice, of course." Barbara salved her pride. "Even Valjenos?"

Barbara nodded. "He likes to play rough." She clicked her teeth together in a playful bite; the lion cub who grows up to be a man-eater. Meow.

"What about Sammy Wuan?"

Barbara's hands stopped describing circles on Jez's back.

"A big man." She emphasized big. "But surprisingly light on his elbows." She smiled. "Not anywhere near as bad as I was expecting."

Then was she ordered to sleep with Sammy Wuan? Jez could guess by whom.

"Too bad Sammy's gone." Barbara pouted.

"Hey!" Jez twisted around, away from Barbara's hands. "Maybe Sammy ran away with the actress I replaced!"

"I don't think so," Barbara said drily. "That girl's dead. You must have read about it, it was in all the papers."

Jez was all blue-eyed innocence. "I don't read the papers." She was glad Toby Cooke wasn't there; that look never got past Dad.

"Oh," Barbara said softly. One hand lightly caressed the carotid artery just below Jez's left ear. The blood there pulsed madly.

"So tense, I could help you." Under her breath, Barbara began to hum. "Christmas is coming," she said coyly.

Jez understood. "I could really use a pick-me-up. These fight scenes are murder." She looked pleadingly at Barbara. "Could you get me something soon?"

"Soon," Barbara promised. "I'll be in touch."

The ex-beauty contestant stroked Jez's hair, coming away with a handful of gold powder; then she walked away, thought better of it, turned back. "I'm so glad you're not going to be like Tina. She was a real stick-in-the-mud." She was gone.

Anger shivered through Jez without warning. She was positive Tina had not been involved with drugs.

She probably hadn't seen anything.

She probably hadn't heard anything.

They'd killed her . . . just in case.

They . . . Valjenos had killed her. The proverbial innocent bystander. Better safe than sorry . . . okay, let's kill her.

Jez was going to get them.

She glanced at her watch . . . five minutes left of lunch break. Just enough time to duck into her dressing room and have a moment's peace all to herself. Five minutes were better than nothing.

She had her hand on the doorknob. She opened it, tensing. Somebody was inside.

Cautiously, Jez peered in. She relaxed; her mysterious intruder was just the play of shadow on a discarded robe. She even laughed a little.

Her laughter was cut short by the raw strength that slammed her against the wall.

She would have fallen except for the rough arm pinned against her neck. "Remember, Miss Nolan," Valjenos said with emotion. "No one here wants to hurt you, unless you make it imperative. If you do . . ." The pressure against her windpipe increased. Her head roared like the ocean in a seashell. "If you do, you can be hurt very easily. After all"— he leaned close, warm breath singing in her ear— "what are you but a small woman, and this is a

man's world." He let go and she flopped to the
ground. "Don't make us hurt you. Barbara would
be so disappointed."

She couldn't stop herself. It felt wrong, being
afraid like this; she was sure the others weren't
afraid. But she couldn't stop herself.

She paused for a second, collecting her thoughts.
What was the name that Micah had told her?

Jez put the coin into the pay phone's slot. She
dialed.

"Hello," said the clear voice that had guided
thousands through the U.N. "I'd like to leave a
message for Mr. Henegan in Room 1601. Dear Steve,
hate military school, the lieutenant's a real killer.
Wish I was home." She coughed, her windpipe
was terribly sore. "Sign it, 'Amanda.' "

Steve Sinclair hated telephone operators and
busboys. He had yet to find a busboy who could
remove a bread basket without showering him with
crumbs.

As for telephone operators, they were in a class
all by themselves.

A very long time ago, Steve had seen a play, not
on Broadway but at some dismal little neighborhood theater. Each character was represented by
two actors, one saying what the character said, the
other saying what he really had on his mind.

Sinclair could just imagine that other Sinclair
answering the operator's clipped request for more
change with searing epithets. "I don't even want
to talk to Marty, much less pay for the privilege!"
Now that was the proper translation of his grunted
"uh-huh."

The operator put his call through.

"Thai TV." The voice had been singsonging those words for so long they had ceased to have meaning.

"Marty Phillips, please. Edit Room C."

"One moment, please." (Translation:—"I wish I could go to lunch already.")

"Edit Room C," another voice announced.

"Marty Phillips, please." (Translation: "Another operator, Goddamn it to hell.")

"Will you hold?"

Steve sighed. "Sure." ("What are my choices?")

"Phillips, here."

"Marty, it's Steve Sinclair . . . don't hang up."

"What do you want? ("What the fuck do you want?")

"We have to talk . . . business." ("I don't like this any more than you do, Phillips.")

"I know . . . the Librarian informed me of your problem." ("Don't think this is a picnic for me either, Steve.")

"When?" ("Cut the shit, Marty.")

"Tonight, my place." ("Fuck you, Steve.")

"All right." ("Fuck you, Marty.")

He hung up the phone, grinning. It was nice to know some people didn't change.

chapter 15

"Isn't this a nice place?" Barbara said happily, gracefully dropping into the chair the waiter held out for her.

Micah looked around the restaurant. It had been Barbara's choice. It was a rather strange choice, but, as he was learning, Barbara was a pretty strange lady.

Rudyard's was a fairly flashy key club. Waitresses decked out in *Jungle Book* costume, waiters in more sedate tuxedos with a tartan slung over one shoulder. The whole place was pretty tacky, but very good-natured about it. It offended about as much as strongly scented deodorant; Micah would rather smell a little honest sweat.

Barbara smelled wonderful. She wore a strapless black sheath, with a pearl choker glowing against her mellow skin. Her hair was loose, swept back from one side of her face with a jeweled clip. She wore no perfume, which surprised and delighted him; her scent was of clean skin and sandalwood.

He could see the skin above one breast pulsing slightly. A strong heart, that was good.

The waiter handed them menus.

"I'm very grateful you accepted my dinner invitation."

She looked at Micah blankly. Her heartbeat did not accelerate. "I mean . . . you don't know me. Not at all."

He put his hand over hers. The menu fluttered like a southern belle's fan. Slowly, her heartbeat picked up. He caught it easily. She'd be a good subject, as long as he kept tap dancing.

Barbara was smiling. "I liked your voice." She peered at him over the top of the menu. "Now, on to more important questions . . . like what are you going to have?" She scanned the menu. "Everything's good here, except the liver." Barbara wrinkled her nose adorably.

Micah decided to see if he could mentally dominate her. "Why don't you have the liver?"

"I hate liver."

"Why don't you have the liver?" He gave her a medium-strength push.

The waiter returned.

Barbara turned to him. "I'll have the liver."

Micah ordered the fish. He really wanted a steak, but he'd discovered that red meat sometimes interfered with his antennae.

The waiter left, taking the menus with him.

That was better; Micah could watch the pupils of her eyes dilate and contract.

"So, Mr. Simmons . . ."

"Michael," he corrected.

"Michael." She colored slightly, pupils dilating. The sign of the open eye. It was a cinch he wasn't going home alone tonight. "What did you want to talk about?"

"I want to produce a film here. But everywhere I go, I get a door slammed in my face. Your boss doesn't seem to have any problems cutting red tape."

"He's very diplomatic. Wins friends and influences people."

"That's some trick." He poured wine for both of them.

She pouted. "All you wanted to do was talk shop?"

"Hardly." He felt her heartbeat zoom. This was no good; he had to stop flirting or he was never going to get a decent reading from her. "I wanted to talk a little insurrection. What would it take to get you to leave Dreamscape and join my team?"

"What are you offering?"

Their dinner came; she dug in with relish; one mental push was good for a long time, it seemed.

"What does Barbara want?"

"I'd like to be Miss Universe," she said softly.

Micah was startled. Take somebody apart and you get sincerity. What he needed was information. "You should be. You're lovely."

She smiled, but her vital signs stayed constant; she'd heard it before, she expected it.

"You know, I don't usually like liver." She put a piece in her mouth. "But this is delicious."

While she was eating, he gave her another tiny push . . . trust me, you know you can trust me. . . . Her breathing relaxed and deepened, a very light suggestive state.

"I'd sure like to know about your boss," he said pleasantly.

Her vitals went haywire. He'd gotten the same reaction asking a failed novitiate about God.

He was going nuts just trying to figure her out.

"Nothing to know . . . from the ridiculous to the sublime." She giggled for no apparent reason.

What the hell does that mean? Micah wondered. "He lost two actors, that's not too bright."

"It's all publicity." Something clicked in her; she was smiling like a toothpaste ad, like she was trying to sell him. "Tina and Sammy were lovers. They had a quarrel and she killed him. The boss hid Sammy's body but Tina ran away." She looked down at her plate. "You read the papers."

He sorted out her reactions: half lie, half truth. But which part? Had Tina killed Sammy? Had they been lovers? Micah had seen pictures of Sammy; he thought it was unlikely.

"You're not a producer, are you?" she said suddenly. He froze. "You're just a smart-ass college kid wasting Daddy's money."

He managed to look offended enough so she'd be positive she'd hit on the truth. "Look, Barbara, can I be honest with you?"

She leaned closer.

He calculated the risk and went for it. "I knew Tina Cooke . . . pretty well."

"Figures she'd get a nice, rich kid like you." Barbara sighed. "Barbara never gets the good guys."

"Your story just doesn't wash, not with me and not with Tina's folks. That's whose money I'm wasting, if you must know."

"I don't need to know!" A few people turned to stare at her outburst. "It's better not to know." Her voice softened. "Look, I like you, I think you're nice, I think you should forget about your old girlfriend and go back to the States. Fast."

No mistaking those signs, she was terrified. She must know what they were capable of, she must know everything. He couldn't let go of her now.

It was tiring, but he gave her one last push . . . I love you, Barbara . . .

Her eyes snapped open.

He didn't feel like too much of a heel. After all, she was one of the bad guys. "I will go back," he promised. "Tomorrow."

When he bent to kiss her, she was there, waiting, and still in wonder.

Valjenos had Jez's purse. It looked a little funny dangling by its strap from his hammy fist, but Jez had no desire to laugh.

The contents of her bag were dumped out onto the dressing-room table. There were lights around the mirror, just like she'd always imagined there'd be.

Telepathy, Jez thought. I'm developing telepathy in my old age. She knew exactly what he was looking at.

Sinclair had told her to remove all her old IDs from her wallet, just in case anybody got curious and was too shy to ask her right to her face. She'd refused to part with one thing. One little nail to secure the lid on her coffin.

It was a picture of her and Tina, arms around each other, taken on a visit back home about a year ago. She couldn't remember exactly when, but that was no problem. Mom liked to write the date on the back of pictures; she liked to write a lot of stuff there.

Jez had kept the picture for good luck.

Some luck.

"Jezebel," Valjenos said. "What a lovely name."

She inched back toward the door and heard the lock click . . . from the outside.

"Jezebel and Tina," he mused. "Lovely names for two lovely sisters."

She swallowed hard. "I don't know what you mean."

"Please don't interrupt me." His tea-party manners were wearing a little thin.

"Sorry." She sat down next to him; anything to forestall him getting a hold on her. She was lost if he did.

"Who sent you here?"

"No one." She looked hurt. "I knew there was something fishy about Tina's death, so I came here to investigate on my own."

"Ahhh." Valjenos considered briefly. "Then you are a very resourceful young woman. Not many American ladies can get a full set of phony identification papers." He leaned close. "Are you as intelligent as you are resourceful?"

She kept quiet. Let him talk, that was the ticket.

"I know you couldn't have arranged this yourself. If you turn in your associates, my . . . superior will be content. In his gratitude, he will hand you over to me. Will you make me hurt you, Miss Cooke, I wonder, or are you smarter than that?"

"I am an American citizen. . . ." she said evenly.

"The cavalry is not here, Miss Cooke. Nor the marines." Outside the door she heard snickering. Valjenos's henchmen.

"We will find your friends." He strode around

her, flipping an imaginery cape over his shoulders "And you will be mine."

He was talking like Basil Rathbone in *Captain Blood*. Except for the fact that this guy was going to rape or kill her shortly, he was a laughable conglomeration of the Late Show and ... Lord D'Arbanville. His master's voice.

If she lived through this, she'd probably get to meet the great man himself.

"Y'know, Juan." Jez's tone was friendly and casual. "I wouldn't mind being yours, except for the fact that I really don't think you can get it up."

As she expected, he charged. She cleared the chair, hoping he'd plow into it.

He didn't. This man had been studying her fighting style. He knew all her tricks.

She advanced, knowing that was the last thing he expected. He dodged her roundhouse punch, laughing. "You can't win, Jezebel."

Keep thinking that, asshole, she thought. Her follow-through carried her to an open container of powder.

She dumped it in Valjenos's eyes, then raced for the small window on the far wall. She could just squeeze through.

A dragon had gotten hold of her legs and was pulling her back inside. The dragon was spitting powder out of its mouth; that was why it wasn't breathing fire.

Far, far, away, outside in the free world, Jez could see Tim Chang, reading a book.

"Tim! Tim!" she screamed, waving her arms wildly.

He waved back.

"Damn you! I'm not waving! Help me!"

Valjenos dragged her back inside. He threw her down on the floor, pinning her under his heavy body.

Kill me or rape me, Jez speculated, amazed at her own calm. Well, if he rapes me, I'm going to kill myself, and I've never been suicidal. Let's see if I can push this bugger over the edge.

He was going to kiss her. She didn't flinch away. When he got close enough she managed to get a good hold on his lip and bit down hard.

He lost what little control he had left and knocked her out cold.

Valjenos looked at the woman on the floor. He started to unbuckle his belt, thought better of it. He wanted her awake, fighting and squirming under him.

He knocked on the door. Ling and Chee, his most trusted goons, entered. They looked at Jez lying there, defenseless.

Valjenos was cleaning his nails with the end of one of Jez's makeup brushes. "You know where to take her."

He saw Chee staring at Jez's breasts. "If you touch her," he added pleasantly, I'll cut off your hands."

Chee bowed respectfully. He knew a good threat when he heard one.

chapter 16

Anchored stolidly in the middle of the lobby, the two antique elevators resembled vigilant eyes. Gleaming brass bars reflected the light. Sinclair pushed a button and an eyelid/car opened to accept him. He pushed another, a gray button numbered six, and it lit up in response. The car closed noisily and began a rackety climb to Marty Phillips's floor, vibrating horizontally while inching along vertically.

The elevator deposited Sinclair directly in front of Marty's door. He buzzed.

"Who is it?"

"Flash from the past." Sinclair groaned inwardly, wished he'd prepared something clever to say.

"Just a second."

The door was opened by a large shapely woman, about Sinclair's own age, with a halo of beige curls and sensuous pouting lips.

"Hello, Marty."

"Hello, Steve."

An awkward silence. The obligatory peck on the cheek, initiated by Marty.

"Come in." She walked away from him, toward a tall, stainless steel and mahogany bar, and Sinclair was afforded a full-length view. What was the expression? Broad where a broad should be broad. "Make yourself comfortable. Vodka martinis all right?"

"Fine."

Sinclair used the opportunity to take in his surroundings. Dark, heavy furniture. Books. A few carvings. Practically bare walls. Most people would have assumed it was a man's apartment. The most prominent pieces were the bookshelves and the bar. Just like Marty, Sinclair mused.

"To old times," she said, handing him a glass.

"To good times," he said.

They drank.

"Sit down," she said.

They did.

"Can we squeeze in a little reminiscing before we get down to business?" She took a long swallow. "I haven't heard from you for a while."

"I . . . dropped out for a few years."

"I'm sorry. I didn't mean for it to sound like an accusation. I don't exactly live in the neighborhood anymore myself." Marty'd been a videotape editor for years. Before that she'd edited film documentaries. Which is what brought her to Thailand in the first place.

Sinclair set his glass down on the low mahogany coffee table. "Why Bangkok?"

"I'm not really sure." She got up, extended her hand. "Refill?" He nodded, handing her his glass. "A film editor has to go where the work is. But that can be pretty lonely. I was working on a project here when the TV station offered me a steady job. I wanted roots. Seemed as good a place as any."

She walked provocatively back to Sinclair, replenished glasses in hand. She moves just like her elevator, he thought, side to side as well as forward. "Maybe this isn't the time for nostalgia," she said, handing him back his glass. "The Librarian mentioned something about Dreamscape Films and a smuggling operation."

"That's right." He took a sip. "Cocaine."

"I guess that makes sense. They certainly couldn't be making money on those schlocky pictures they turn out."

He chuckled. "We assume that the drugs are being transported in the cans of film."

"Could be. Opening or X-raying a film can would destroy the contents. So cans are usually allowed to go through security without inspection."

"What we don't know is how the drops are being made. The main reason this operation has been so successful is that the merchandise is never distributed in the same place twice."

She thought for a minute. "That information must be in the cans, too. Probably on the film itself. Right?"

"That's what I'm here to ask you."

"Oh. Right. Of course." She laughed throatily and rested her hand on his knee. He pretended not to notice. "Let me see. Another drink?"

"Not for me."

"Suit yourself." She rose and crossed again, though more slowly this time, to the large shining bar.

"It could be visual." She poured as she talked. "Locations in the film which correspond to places in the various cities where the drops are to be made."

Sinclair considered for a moment, then shook his head. "Too risky. Anybody watching the movie might make the connection, by chance."

"Yeah." She crinkled her nose. "Expensive, too. Dreamscape doesn't have the facilities to build such elaborate sets. Well ..." She kicked off her shoes, and started back toward the couch where Sinclair was sitting, "There's the script. Places could be concealed in the dialogue."

"Uh-uh. Same problem. A casual viewer, or an agent, could hear the name of a familiar place in his city, and put two and two together."

"Not necessarily. The films are all shot in English and Thai, then dubbed into various languages before distribution. If the dealers were bilingual, they could spot a discrepancy between the actors' lips on the screen and the voice dubbed over, especially if they were looking for it."

"Sounds too complicated."

She shrugged. "You said it was a very successful operation." She settled into the couch next to Sinclair, the back of her head against a cushion.

"Okay." She let out a long deep sigh.

Sinclair ran his hand over his mouth thoughtfully and left it propping up his chin. "What if ..."

"Subliminal images."

"Hm?"

"Subliminal images." She sat up, her forehead creased in thought. She opened her mouth, turned to Sinclair, and raised a finger. Then, "No, it's too farfetched," she scoffed, and leaned back against the cushion again.

"What?" Sinclair asked insistently.

"Well, subliminal images."

"What are they?"

"Frames of film, pictures, interspersed with the real movie. They used to be very popular with advertisers in the States, until they were outlawed. A box of popcorn every fifty frames of film, say. You wouldn't actually consciously see the popcorn, but subconsciously . . ."

"The image is planted in your brain."

"Right." She frowned. "Of course, a person wouldn't be able to pick up a location consciously by watching the film."

An idea suddenly dawned in Sinclair's mind. "But if the dealer was a theater owner . . ."

"Or a projectionist." She shook her head. "No, no, it's just too crazy."

"Just crazy enough to work," Sinclair said. "Where's your phone?"

"There's an extension in the bedroom," Marty answered, pointing toward a dark corridor.

He found the phone without too much trouble. Flicking on a lamp over the night table where it sat, he dialed the hotel.

"Good evening, Embassy Hotel," chirped a too cheerful voice.

"Room 1603, please."

"Hold on, sir. I'll connect you." Six rings. No answer. Micah was probably still out with that continuity girl, Barbara Tiang.

The cheerful voice came back. "Room 1603 doesn't answer, sir."

"No kidding."

"I beg your pardon?"

"Nothing." Try Jez. "Could you try 1605 please, operator?"

"Of course, sir." Sinclair heard a slight edge in the voice this time.

More rings. No answer. Sinclair didn't wait to be assaulted again by the sugarplum fairy. He hung up.

He reached up to turn off the lamp. A warm hand stopped him. "Don't turn out the light," Marty whispered in his ear. "I hate to be undressed in the dark." Her tongue followed her voice.

"Martina Phillips," Sinclair said in a low chiding tone, "you think, talk, and act like a man."

"Ah," she said, biting his ear. "But I make love like a woman."

"I haven't seen you in such a long while, I can't remember."

"Then it's definitely time for a refresher course."

He turned around to face her, their hands still touching. She kissed him hotly on the lips, her tongue darting around inside his mouth.

Sinclair unbuttoned her white silk blouse slowly, lightly kissing the newly exposed flesh after each unbuttoning.

She wore a lacy white bra. It barely contained the amplitude of her creamy breasts. When Sinclair undid the front clasp, they spilled out into his hands, as if in greeting. He caressed and kissed them repeatedly, gently teasing the pinkish-brown nipples until they stood erect. She began to moan and sigh softly, her fingernails running up and down his back encouragingly.

He wrapped one arm around her narrow waist, placed the other behind her knees, and lifted her up and onto the king-sized bed. She lay very still, her breath coming in short, excited gasps. He knelt above her on the black satin bedspread.

Gently he inserted his thumbs beneath the elasticized waistband of her white slacks and pulled. He did it slowly, enjoying each portion of her silky body as it was revealed. He'd forgotten how smooth and lustrous her skin was.

First her thighs came into view, large but firm, round, and well muscled. Then her knees, calves, ankles, and finally her tiny feet. She wore white luminous nail polish on her toes.

Her panties were also lacy and white. A hint of brown hair peeked from the sides. He ran his hand over the front slowly and heavily, as if probing the curly triangle beneath.

"Oh, God, rip them off," she moaned.

He did.

She reached up and unhooked his belt.

He turned off the lamp.

"Spoilsport," she said.

"Better than I remembered," she said.

He kissed her forehead and fondled her firm ass with gentle strokes.

"Steve?"

"Mm?"

"Thank you."

"For what?"

"Would you laugh if I said for making me feel like a woman?"

"Am I laughing?"

She kissed his shoulder and began making circular motions with her finger over the curly black hairs on his chest. "I . . . I'm sorry about Amanda."

He stiffened under her touch. "What does that have to do with us?"

"Maybe nothing, maybe a lot." She took a deep breath. "I'm thinking of moving back to the States."

"Good. You've been living like a nun too long."

"Look who's talking." She gave his chest hair a playful tug. Her voice went back to a serious tone. "I didn't settle in Bangkok because I wanted roots. I was running away. From a man. Or several." She paused. "I drink too much," she added incongruously.

"I'm not sure what you expect me to say."

"Oh, neither am I. Welcome back? Call me when you get in? Fuck you?"

"All right, Scarlett, welcome back, call me when you get in." He kissed her long and hard. "And fuck you."

"Marty?"

"Mm?"

"I have to go now."

"Oh, Steve." Her voice was somewhere between a growl and a whimper.

She wound her arms more tightly around him.

Even if I didn't have to, I'd want to, he thought, then hated himself for thinking it.

He kissed each of her hands tenderly, then disengaged himself from her grasp.

"Good-bye," she said, and rolled over.

Sinclair smiled. Definitely a survivor, he thought. He got out of bed quietly and fumbled around in the dark for his clothes.

He carried his bundle of clothes out into the living room and laid them on the bar. Turning on a small goose-necked lamp to see by, he began to dress. His eyes caught sight of a telephone concealed beneath the smooth wood surface of the bar top. He remembered Marty pointing him to the phone in the bedroom and shook his head. Like a man, he thought, just like a man.

He wrote her a note, which included his address and phone number in the states, and laid it on the bar under the empty vodka bottle.

He left.

The cool night was refreshing, a surprising contrast to the swelter of the day. Sinclair strolled to the corner, taking in the starry sky, the neon signs, the petite, colorful dressed women. He looked around, expecting to see at least a few GIs, then suddenly remembered he wasn't in Saigon. Sleepy.

He reached up his hand to hail a *samlor* and saw that he had forgotten his watch. Shit, he thought. After all that rigamarole I went through to make a smooth gentlemanly exit. Ah, well, maybe Ms. Phillips will be up and ready for another round, he thought wryly, and headed back for her apartment house.

The desk clerk was nodding off, so Sinclair trod carefully past him to the two-eyed elevator. He pushed the button, then looked up to see which floors the cars were on. Three and six. Marty's floor.

As the nearer car reached the first floor and opened, the other seemed to descend in a wink. Sinclair heard it hit the ground floor as his own car started to ascend.

Again the slow, rackety vibrating climb.

Marty's door was unlocked, as he'd left it. He turned the knob as quietly as he could and carefully opened the door. The rest of the apartment was dark, but bright light came from the beddroom. So much for stealth.

"Hey! Anybody seen a big brunette with perfect knockers?" he called out in a mock-thug voice.

No answer.

He walked briskly to the bedroom, stopped cold in the doorway.

Marty lay faceup on the bed, naked in a pool of her own blood. Her throat was slashed. Her face, breasts, and thighs bore the marks of D'Arbanville's ring.

Sinclair dashed to the elevator, pushed the button, waited what seemed like an eternity for the car to come, another eternity to ride to the lobby.

He ran out of the building into the street knowing he was too late, knowing D'Arbanville must have been riding down in the winking elevator car as he was boarding the other, knowing how close he'd been.

He turned back to the lobby. Both eyelid/cars rested on the ground floor.

See no evil.

chapter 17

"Damn," Barbara said faintly.

She'd turned the hall light on and it blew. For a second, they'd been in light, then "pop," and the darkness returned.

Micah did not mind it, but from the way Barbara had reached in the front door, grabbing for that light switch like a life preserver, he assumed she was frightened of the dark.

She was trying to fumble her way down the hall to the next light switch without much success. He heard her bark her shin on something, probably a low table. Geez, lady, Micah thought, this is *your* apartment. "Have you got a lighter?"

"Wha?"

"In your purse," he explained. "Have you got one?"

She handed him a small, flat lighter. It felt expensive. The little flame illuminated her face, her very relieved face. She smiled wanly. "Guess I don't like the dark very much."

He felt the trembling pressure of her hand on his.

185

He blew the little flame out.

"Don't!" she wailed, clinging to him. Micah thought of all the monster movies he'd seen as a teenager: remembering all those wonderful, shrieking girls clinging to his arm (muscular arm, they would tell their friends later) every time that monster showed his latex face. He still loved monster movies.

Micah kissed Barbara gently. She seemed a little puzzled; maybe she was expecting the mad rapist, but Micah was in no hurry. He had his own way of doing things.

In high school, he never had to beg a girl to go all the way, like other boys. He merely kissed the girls into submission, until finally they'd scream, "Do it already!" He never touched a girl who didn't want to be touched. He never begged or coerced. He just took his time.

In college, a trio of witty co-eds dubbed him "Slowhand." His roommate assumed he played guitar. He did not. He did not have time.

Barbara shifted, gluing herself to him from her knees to her breasts. Her hands resting on his shoulders very lightly, just fingertips, really. He leaned against the wall, feeling her weight against him. She was so light, she was a butterfly. Madame Butterfly.

He chuckled softly and she looked up, her mouth glistening with his own mouth's wetness.

"What are you thinking about?"

"Puccini."

She didn't understand. So she just held her face up to his for a little more mouth-to-mouth. He was happy to oblige. One hand clutched his shoulder a little compulsively. They broke.

"God, please," she whispered. "You're killing me." She squirmed against him. "Do something."

Easily, he cradled her in his arms, took a step forward. "Uh, Barbara, you got a bed around here?"

She was disoriented. "It's here somewhere."

He forged ahead bravely, lips still fastened to Barbara's and hit something pretty solid. Teak, Micah guessed. Beside him, Madame Butterfly flew through the air and landed with a sharp "thok."

"Owww."

"Barbara?" He started crawling toward her in the dark.

"I hit my head on the telephone . . . yeow!" He'd stepped on her.

"Sorry." Then he ran into the nightstand. At least they were near the bed. Hanging on to each other, they clambered up.

Micah flopped over onto his back; Barbara lay next to him in the same position. They both looked up at where they assumed the ceiling was. This had to be the darkest apartment he'd ever been in.

"Has the wind gone out of your sails?" she asked innocently.

He didn't answer. Never had he spent so much energy for so little.

"Never mind, just leave everything to me." Her manner changed, as she adopted the role of courtesan. How many times had she played that part on D'Arbanville's orders?

He's just like all the others, Barbara told herself as she slithered down the length of his body. All men are the same. Selfish.

Micah grabbed her wrists and hauled her up until they were nose to nose. "I know this is your ballroom," he said, "but do you mind if I lead?"

She did not.

She giggled, at first weakly, then with more conviction. "At least you college boys have a sense—"

"Shut up, Barbara," he said, kissing her. "Shhh."

The black sheath had slipped down just to the top of her nipples. Grazing on her neck and earlobes, he slid his fingertips across the swell of her breasts, feeling for the zipper. It ran down the side, the designer being unwilling to spoil the lovely line of smooth fabric falling over silken buttocks.

The dress slipped to her tiny waist, catching on the fuller width of her hips. She didn't have a stitch on underneath. With teeth and tongue, he followed the trail made by smooth muscle, curving from her underarm, down around to her breast, cupping his hand there, feeling the warm weight.

"Ah," Barbara breathed.

Ah, you've got a lovely opera there, Mr. Puccini.

Ah, you've got a lovely bunch of coconuts.

"Ah." He felt Barbara's light touch on his shoulders stripping the shirt from his body, tugging at his belt. Her breathing quickened as her desire increased and she pulled him down to her warm, pearly flesh. Her eager mouth was everywhere, lips, eyelids, chest, fingertips. Silken hair trailed his stomach. Butterfly kisses on his groin.

Groaning, he gathered her into his arms. Like magic, her thighs parted as her legs wrapped around him. He had forgotten to take off her shoes and one slim heel rubbed against his thigh. He entered her, dipping into her like smooth candy, teasing, exploring. The pressure of her legs locked around him, tightened, driving him deeper, imploring him to thrust harder, faster.

He curved one hand around her furiously pumping ass, leading her into his rhythm, riding her just to the brink, once, twice, a hundred sweetly agonizing little deaths before he finally took her over the edge, falling with her. One hand worked convulsively, snagged on her necklace. Dimly, he heard the splash of pearls spilling over the bed and onto the floor.

"I've always depended on my looks to get me by," Barbara was saying. "It's only lately I've begun to realize they won't be here forever."

"Oriental women age gracefully."

"But they age." She smiled ruefully. "Ugly girls have to develop their minds, but pretty girls just coast. Why do you think I got mixed up with such a bad lot? I could tell you some pretty crazy stories. . . ."

He wished she would, but he was too tired to give her another mental push. "You could get out, Barbara." he said softly.

"What would I do? I can't type and my tastes are too expensive for the government to support me. I could peddle my ass on the boulevard and not do as well as I do now. I may be a whore, but I'm not a stupid one."

"Dreamscape is going to blow up right in their faces. Do you want to be around for that?"

She sighed in the dark. "I no longer believe that the good guys win or that crime doesn't pay. Look around you, you better believe it pays. I'm comfortable here, and too lazy to change my ways now." She turned toward him. "Tell me, are you really any different than I am?"

"I am different," he whispered, more for his benefit than hers. "I am not like you."

* * *

Jez breathed deeply, rapidly. Struggled for breath. She couldn't remember being this exhausted, ever. Tina hadn't exaggerated about the strenuousness of these fight scenes.

Valjenos shouted something unintelligible, and Jez's opponent stepped forward, seemingly out of nowhere.

Somebody called him Lodar—archfiend and sworn enemy of the Circle of Eight, Jez supposed, smirking. He wore oriental pajamas, a white bowler, and a lot of makeup. The cheeks were red, the grinning mouth redder. Mascara, eyeliner, and silver eyeshadow liberally adorned eyes that sparkled like highly polished diamonds.

Jez shuddered and assumed the stance Valjenos had shown her.

Somebody yelled action, and Jez struck. The blow was clumsily executed, but it connected. Lodar collapsed in a heap at her feet. Just like a Chinese lantern, Jez thought.

Her hands felt so stiff she could barely flex them. Her arms were like lead.

Lodar writhed up slowly like a snake to meet her, the maniacal grin still in place. What's next? she thought, panicky. Am I supposed to hit him again?

She couldn't remember, so she did. He went down again, more quickly than before. The bowler toppled off his head and floated to the floor, where it whirled, making a drumroll sound.

Jez twisted and rolled her shoulders, trying to loosen them up.

The figure rose sinuously again; the face wasn't

Lodar. It was Valjenos. He had the same smug expression, the same exaggerated painted face.

He was shouting something at her, but she couldn't make out what he was saying. He was furious, spitting out words. "My decision, something-something, always prevent, something-something, too soft, something-something, stay in line."

She wanted to tell him to slow down so she could understand; she'd try to do what he was telling her to, but she was afraid he'd get angrier.

And she was too tired to fight him again. She opened her mouth to speak; nothing came out.

She tried again; nothing.

Valjenos was still shouting, draining all the energy from her body.

He was suddenly very far away, yelling at another person—Lodar?—about her. He said her name several times.

The person Valjenos was yelling at was arguing back, matching him phrase for phrase. It was a man, Jez thought. He had a silky mellifluous voice. Sounds, slidding up and down the scale, with a sensual intensity behind them. No, not sensual. Creepy.

Evil.

There was a sudden silence. The bowler still whirled on the floor in front of her.

Then a powerful bellow—"MINE!"—which jolted her . . . awake.

She opened her eyes sluggishly. Blurry splashes of color surrounded by pitchy black,

"You repeatedly undermine my authority with the locals," Valjenos was screaming.

"If your 'authority' was based on respect and

nor fear, Juan," the other responded smoothly, "it would not be so easily undermined."

"Stop trying to confuse me with your . . ." He faltered. Jez could hear him hyperventilating. "Your drawing room logic! Respect is for equals, like you and I. I am the one who leads the workers, day to day. I cannot keep order if you insist on overruling me. I must rule unquestioned."

The other brayed uncontrollably. "I am sorry to disillusion you, Juan, but Thailand is no banana republic and you are not its dictator. Even the most unsophisticated of our dealers considers this a business, which it is, and not a crusade." He laughed again, derisively.

At that instant, Jez knew it was D'Arbanville. Her body went numb with fear. Then she felt a constriction in her throat as if she was going to throw up. She remembered why she was here, the tragedy that had brought her to Thailand, and loathing, rage, replaced the feeling of nausea. All right, now wake up and do what you came here to do.

Her hands and feet were tied with thin black nylon cord to the chair she was sitting in. Obviously the Valjenos touch, she thought sourly.

They were only a few feet away, but in virtual darkness. She sat directly under a hot white bulb, its spill giving her her only glimpse of them. She dared not move or open her eyes too wide, but she listened.

Valjenos seemed to be losing steam. D'Arbanville was talking. His speech was overly precise and measured, as if he were giving Valjenos an English lesson.

"You only captured Miss Cooke to reinforce your

drooping machismo. Admit it and be done with it, Juan."

"She is a spy." His voice was building again, into another tirade. "She lied, and attempted to extort information. She was out to destroy us."

"Perhaps I should reintroduce the firing squad," D'Arbanville said dryly. "Single-handed?"

"What?"

"Was she plotting our destruction alone, as she claimed, or working with others?"

"Others?"

D'Arbanville emitted a low growl. "One, two, three, four, five, six, seven, eight, nine . . ." He chuckled throatily. "Ten, you really are amazingly obtuse at times. Others bent on our destruction. Other spies, another organization attempting to encroach upon our territory, personal enemies. Others."

"I—I don't know, sir."

"Precisely. And neither do I. And now we have no way of finding out unless we torture her, which we don't want to do since you, and I incidentally, have other things in mind for her superb anatomy."

"I beg your pardon?"

"That's right, Juan. Play dumb. Then I won't be as angry with you. Now the correct thing to have done, after discovering that the actress Sheri Nolan was actually the snoop Jezebel Cooke, was nothing. Had you left her alone and kept a close watch on her, you might also have discovered the identities of her associates, if any.

"Instead, there she sits, an adorable albatross around your neck, although I fancy you picture her dangling from a lower part of your person. Are you blushing or fuming, Juan? You look like a ripe tomato."

Jez heard no reply, but footsteps sounded closer and closer. She fought hard against the urge to open her eyes and see D'Arbanville face-to-face.

"Nevertheless," he said, directly above her, "we must deal with the problem at hand instead of crying over spilt milk. What do you propose to do with your delectable prize, now that you have so impetuously confiscated it?"

She heard Valjenos clomp in her direction. He stopped very near.

A large hand began firmly caressing her hair.

"She is incomparable." Valjenos. It was probably his hand, too.

"And," D'Arbanville added, "she is, thus far, unviolated by you. After you have exercised your Latin libido on her a few times, you'll willingly put her on the street, sell her into white slavery, or turn her into dog food."

"Perhaps," Valjenos countered evasively. "But for now I'm content to, as you say, 'exercise' on her. I just bought some excruciating new bedroom tools with the leggy Jezebel"—he clutched a handful of her hair—"specifically in mind."

"I'm sorry, Juan," D'Arbanville murmured, sounding not in the least sorry, "but I have plans of my own for Miss Cooke. When I'm finished, there might be a few pieces of her left for you to play with."

* * *

Barbara was a light sleeper.

She heard the phone ringing in the dark apartment. She didn't think it strange that someone would call her at two o'clock in the morning. Lots of people did. She simply did not want to wake her guest, Joe College.

The phone rang again. In his well-deserved sleep, Micah turned over on his side.

Barbara looked at him, smiling. An old lover had told her she could make a fortune billing herself as a cure for insomnia.

She slipped out of bed and got to the phone before it rang again.

"Hello, loser," Valjenos snarled. "It appears your friend Sheri Nolan is a fake. Her real name is Cooke. Understand. Lord D. will be very disappointed in you."

Barbara shivered. The last thing she wanted was to incur Valjenos's wrath. He was Lord D.'s lapdog, and God knows what would happen if they both came down on her.

"It's not my fault," she whimpered. "I checked her out, I played up to her like you told me. She lied to me, too. She told me she was a user; I was sure she was on the level."

"I haven't time for you now, Barbara." His voice was coldly hollow through the telephone. "We'll find out where her friends are hiding and then . . . well, a lot of things could happen to her . . . and you."

"I'll make it up to you, Juan," she whispered. "You know I will."

He laughed. "I know you will try, dear Barbara. But will you succeed? Who can say?" The line went dead.

Her mind started racing like a caged rat. The best thing was to get out of the country, fast. She spun around.

Micah was there. He'd put on his trousers though he was still barefoot. She hadn't heard him at all.

What did that matter, though. What could half a phone conversation mean to him?

Barbara did not know how very, very keen Micah's hearing was. She did not know he recognized Valjenos's voice from the audition hall.

"Where is she?"

"Go back to bed."

He caught her arm. "Where are they keeping Jezebel?"

Her eyes flew open. "You're working together."

"Where is she?" He grabbed the other arm, immobilizing her.

Barbara laughed. "You won't kill me, you won't even hurt me, hey, Mr. White Hat Good Guy?"

"You're right, I won't hurt you." He smiled, stroking her tangled hair. "But I will see to it you rot in jail. If Jez dies, you might even get fried for murder one."

She gasped. "What do you want to do that for? I got money, lots of it. I like you, you like me; we could forget all this shit, go away someplace together."

He slapped her. It startled both of them. "I told you, I am not like you. Now, where is she?"

"I don't know."

She was lying. He started to dial the police.

"No!" She flung herself on the phone, nestling it to her body. "It's a secret place. You'll never find it, even if I direct you."

"Sure I'll find it, Barbara." He pulled her to her feet. " 'Cause you're coming with me."

chapter 18

Sinclair spent two hours with the Bangkok police.
First showing them Marty's mutilated body, then
confirming her identity, then his own.

"Yes, they'd had an appointment.

"Yes, they were old friends.

No, he hadn't killed her.

Yes, he knew who did.

No, he didn't know where to find him.

Yes, it must have happened right after he left
Marty's apartment the first time.

Bangkok's finest. Sinclair didn't know whether
to laugh or throw up.

The police lieutenant who questioned him, a Mr.
Hyun, had obviously been weaned on Charlie Chan
movies and still watched the Perry Mason reruns
on Thai TV. He paced thoughtfully as he conducted
his investigation, smacking his lips open before
each question, pausing significantly and turning
on Sinclair near the end.

Smack. "So, Mr. Sinclair, you say that you left
Miss Phillips's apartment at approximately eleven

197

P.M., returning some fifteen or so minutes later to retrieve"—pause, turn—"a wristwatch you had left behind."

"That's right."

Begin pacing again. Smack. "During which time, one Richard D'Arbanville slipped in, killed and mutilated her, and"—pause, turn—"slipped out again."

"Bingo."

Begin pacing again, with gusto. Loud smack. "How is it then that the desk clerk saw neither your departure and reentry nor that of the phantom Lord D'Arbanville." Pause. Turn. Smack, smack. "And how, furthermore, when you yourself have admitted that you left your wristwatch behind, are you able to so precisely pinpoint the times of these alleged events?" Crescendo. Wipe brow with handkerchief.

Sinclair considered applauding but feared Hyun might do an encore. Instead he said, "I have a friend who can straighten out this entire matter. May I use your phone?"

Hyun was incredulous but affected nonchalance. "By all means."

"Thank you."

The expression on the police lieutenant's face was priceless when Sinclair began unscrewing the mouthpiece on the desk phone, replacing it with his own. Hyun's face registered confusion, then astonishment, and finally piggish anger. Sinclair told him to get on the extension and he did, just as the Librarian came on the line.

"Steve?"

"Yes, sir?"

"The gulf winds have suddenly turned colder."

"But it won't stop the pink salmon from swimming upstream," Sinclair answered sourly. He had no trouble remembering the code responses this time. Hyun looked as if he was ready to call in a psychiatrist.

"I assume you have made contact with Marty Phillips?"

"Yes."

"Was she able to speculate on how the drops are being made?"

"We think we have a good idea."

"Splendid. Miss Phillips is one of our most astute and cooperative friends in the Far East."

"Was."

"I beg your pardon?"

"D'Arbanville killed her." He let it hang, resonate on the line, before continuing. "When he was through with her, she looked like Tina Cooke's identical twin."

There was a long silence. Finally the Librarian spoke, not a trace of officiousness or patronizing in his voice. Simply, "I'm sorry, Steve."

"I know you are."

"There's nothing you could have done to prevent this. If Marty Phillips was marked by D'Arbanville, her death was inevitable."

"I know." He tried to sound like he believed it.

"Just be grateful that you were able to reach her before he did. I'm sure her last few hours were very pleasurable, spent with an old friend." A fleeting image of the two of them in bed together crossed Sinclair's mind. "Thanks to Miss Phillips, we'll be able to shut down D'Arbanville's Thai operation permanently."

"Yeah. There's one other thing," he said, eager to change the subject.

"Yes. What?" the Librarian countered, just as eager.

Sinclair stole a glance at Hyun, who was listening intently on the extension, eyes agog. "The police here think I may have killed Marty. I'm being held as a witness, pending, I assume, arrest."

Hyun looked guiltily over at Sinclair, who was waiting for it. He gave the lieutenant his best you-are-in-a-shitload-of-trouble stare. Embarrassment slowly crept into Hyun's complexion.

"Oh, I'll take care of that right away," the Librarian said. "Good-bye, Steve."

"Good-bye."

"Good luck with the rest of the mission."

"Right." The line went dead.

Sinclair replaced the mouthpiece to the tune of Hyun nervously smacking his lips about a dozen times.

A minute or two passed during which Hyun noisily shuffled papers around his desk, avoiding but intensely feeling Sinclair's steely gaze.

The phone rang. Hyun swooped up the receiver before the first ring was completed, and a series of "yes, sir's," "no, sir's," and "uh-huhs" followed. The conversation ended with a low "right away, sir."

Gathering his papers, and likewise his dignity, into a neat little pile, Hyun rose from his desk and spoke, his voice oozing sincerity. "Terribly sorry to have detained you, Mr. Sinclair." Smack. "I'll send a squad car around to take you back to the hotel."

"Right," Sinclair said. "Right."

"No hard feelings, I hope." Smack. "Just trying to do my job." Hyun extended a sweaty hand.

Sinclair accepted it. "Yeah, me too," he said, almost inaudibly.

It was 2:30 when the squad car deposited Sinclair under the awning of the Embassy Hotel. The street were deserted. A light rain fell. He walked through the tinted-glass door and into the lobby.

Better leave a wake-up call, he thought. Don't want a repeat of yesterday morning. He approached the desk.

The night clerk was a sleepy, bespectacled girl who outweighed Sinclair by a good hundred pounds. Her face was buried in a paperback copy of *The Shining*. Her jaws methodically worked over a large wad of chewing gum.

"Miss?" No answer. A little louder. "Miss?"

The face looked up dully from the book.

Sorry to distrub your grazing, Sinclair thought. "I'd like to leave a wake-up call," he said. Her eyes didn't change expression. Her mouth kept chewing. "My name's Henegan and I'm in Room—"

"You have a message," she said in a low monotone.

Sinclair nodded slowly, then gave her a thirty-two-tooth smile. "I beg your pardon?"

"You have a message," she said again, in exactly the same voice.

Is it live or Memorex, he thought, still smiling.

She handed him a pink slip of paper, folded twice.

"Thanks," he said, and winked at her, pulling the message out of a cluster of sausage fingers.

Her head dropped back into the book.

Yawning, Sinclair unfolded the note. Just get me to bed, he thought.

Its contents brought him awake like a hard slap: "DearSteve hate military school the lieutenant's a real killer"—KILLER—"wish I was home . . . Amanda."

He knocked hard on the desk twice to get the clerk's attention. "What time did this message come in?"

"I dunno. It was here when I got here at eleven." Chomp, chomp.

"Ring Room 1605 for me, please."

"It's after midnight." Chomp, chomp. "I cannot ring guests after midnight."

"It's 2:38." He leaned over the desk, knuckles white, pressing the top. "And if you don't ring this guest for me, I'm going to take that paperback book you're holding in your fat fingers, and turn it into an enema."

Her eyes widened into saucers, her mouth contracted into a button, and she rang Room 1605.

Six rings. No answer. "The guest is not answering, sir."

"Try 1603."

"But . . ."

He snatched the book out of her hands. "Try 1603."

She did.

Where the fuck is Jez, he wondered. Why had she signed the message "Amanda"? Maybe it wasn't from her at all. This whole stinking wild-goose chase was starting to remind him a lot of London.

"No answer in 1603, either, sir," the clerk said, just as the house phone rang. "Good morning, Embassy Hotel."

Sinclair started for the elevator. Call the Librarian for an update. Then load up and look for Jez.

He heard the clerk saying, "No, I told you before. Room 1601 is not in. You should try in the morning. Now . . ."

"Hey!" Sinclair boomed.

The clerk stopped talking and held the receiver against her chest protectively. She began biting her nails as he walked back to the desk.

Sinclair's hands reached out, stretched into a choking gesture, but his voice was calm and soft, almost a whisper. "I," he said, "am 1601."

She reacted as if he had said "Jack the Ripper," clutching more tightly and biting more fiercely.

He touched the receiver gently, then jerked it out of her hand in one motion. She gasped, then started to cry, her entire upper body shaking uncontrollably. Sinclair gave her back her book, and she plodded, blubbering, to the ladies' room.

"Yeah," Sinclair said into the phone.

"It's Micah. Did you just get in?"

"Yeah. Where are you?"

"I'm at Barbara Tiang's apartment."

Barbara Tiang's apartment. He should have known. "Have you heard from Jez?"

"Uh, sort of. That's what I'm calling about." Micah let out a deep sigh.

"What, am I supposed to guess?"

"No, no. Sorry, Sinclair. It's just been a very weird night."

Sorry. Christ, how many times had he heard that in the last few hours?

Micah went on. "Valjenos called a few minutes ago. He's got Jez."

"Are you sure?"

"Uh-huh. Her cover's blown. Somehow he overpowered her. He . . . just a minute."

Sinclair could faintly hear a female voice on the other end of the line. Micah came back on. "Barbara says he's a first-class S-and-M freak. Sounds bad."

Sinclair looked down at the pink note he held. "It is," he said. "Do you know where they are?"

"Barbara does. She'll show us how to get there."

"Fine." Cozy, he thought.

"Oh, and Sinclair?"

"Yeah?"

"I think I know how Dreamscape makes the drops."

"Look, we can compare notes in the car. Let's just get moving, okay?"

"Yeah. We'll pick you up in about ten minutes." He hung up.

Sinclair lifted the note to eye level and stared at it. The words "killer" and "Amanda" seemed to jump off the page at him.

The door to the ladies' room opened, and the desk clerk's head peeked out, followed by the rest of her. She walked toward the hotel desk as if she had blinders on, head erect and a little ahead of the body. Her feet took mincing steps, her hands tugged at the hem of her orange T-shirt.

"What's your name?" Sinclair asked her.

"Geni," she muttered.

"Geni," Sinclair said, "I'm sorry I frightened you."

Geni's eyes darted around as if looking for the hidden camera.

"You ought to smile more."

This caused her to try. The result was pretty abysmal. Kind of a squint, and a jagged one at that. "Did you want to leave a wake-up call, Mr. Henegan?" she asked, in an almost pleasant voice.

"No," Sinclair said. He crumpled the pink note into a ball and shot it into a wastebasket near her feet. "I just got it."

It was still raining, a little harder. Sinclair stood under the protective awning and waited. No people on the street, and a very few cars passing by.

About three blocks up, a small car was screeching through a particularly wide right turn. It jerked into its own lane after making the corner and barreled loudly down the street in Sinclair's direction.

He smiled, knowingly. Who else? When the car, which turned out to be a canary-yellow Subaru, ground to a halt at the hotel entrance, Sinclair saw, however, that he was only half right. Micah sat in the front passenger's seat, and the driver of the vehicle was a beautiful black-haired, black-eyed oriental.

"Meet Barbara Tiang," Micah said, opening a curbside door for Sinclair.

The woman smiled. "Luscious" was the first word that came to Sinclair's mind.

He got in. "Where is it that we're going?"

"Valjenos's headquarters," Barbara said. "He calls it the Lair."

"At Dreamscape Films?"

"Oh, no. This is a bit more private. Juan likes to have a separate suite of offices away from the studio."

Micah and Sinclair exchanged a look.

"Why?"

"I don't know," she said simply. "He's an unusual, complex man with his share of quirks."

"I think he got a triple dose," Micah said.

"Hm?"

"Just offices?" Sinclair asked.

"Well, actually it's more like a warehouse. Lots of rooms. Some for storage, some for entertaining potential investors, Juan's suite of offices. And there's a restaurant in front."

"In front, huh?"

"Mm-hm."

Micah nudged Sinclair. "Are you thinking what I'm thinking?" he asked, sotto voce.

"If I'm not, one of us should go back to spy school." Aloud, Sinclair said, "All that in one building. Huh. From the ridiculous to the sublime."

Barbara laughed. "Funny," she said.

"What?"

"That's Juan's favorite phrase. He says it all the time."

"No kidding."

Micah nudged Sinclair again. "That's what I started to tell you on the phone. It's . . ."

"Subliminal images. I know."

"How'd you figure it out?"

"Marty."

"Oh, yeah. How'd that go?"

"Fine. Got what I wanted. So did D'Arbanville."

"How's that?"

"Marty and Tina Cooke are roommates now."

Silence. "I'm sorry. You two guys went back a long time, huh?"

"Yup."

Barbara drove the yellow Subaru into a diagonal parking space and turned off the engine. "Well, we're here," she said.

Micah looked out the window and got an unpleasant surprise. "Rudyard's," he muttered sheepishly.

chapter 19

RUDYARD'S.

The huge neon sign flashed red, then white, then blue.

"The colors of our national flag," Barbara said.

"Good choice," Sinclair said.

He walked a little way behind Micah and Barbara, taking it all in. Brick, wood paneling, stucco, and stone slapped helter-skelter on the building's three-story facade. Artificial shrubs in Crayola colors stuck into wood chips running all the way around. A purple dragon, seven feet tall and twice as long guarded the entrance, its red plaster tongue hanging down like an exhausted dog's.

"Class," Sinclair said.

"With a capital K," Micah said.

The entrance was a fluorescent red door recessed in a brightly lit archway. The archway was decorated with drawings of scantily clad, well-endowed girls and swirls of psychedelic color.

"It's like being inside a pinball machine," Sinclair muttered.

Barbara knocked several times, hard. A rectangular hole opened in the door, a pair of slanted eyes peered out.

"They've got to be kidding," Sinclair said.

"Wait'll you see the inside," Micah said.

Barbara shoved a fifty-baht bill through the rectangular hole, and the red door opened.

It was Micah's turn to be surprised. Rudyard's the tourist-trap restaurant had become Rudyard's the tourist-trap casino. The garish red-and-gold-brocade wallpaper remained, but the small round dining tables had been replaced by large rectangular ones with red felt tops, the *Jungle Book* waitresses and tartaned waiters by voluptuous croupiers in tight evening gowns and burly bouncers in black dinner jackets. Micah thought he had seen some of the men hanging around the studio the day of Jez's audition.

A massive crystal chandelier hung in the center of the room. Underneath it was a mahogany octagon, topped with black velvet. The piece was solid, save for a small hole in the middle where a dealer presently stood. Edged in silver, it reminded Sinclair of Marty Phillips's bar.

"Star table?" he asked Barbara.

She nodded.

Seated around it were a florid-faced bald man getting tips from a cotton-candy blond with pink lipstick; a wet-headed Latin with a paisley shirt unbuttoned to the navel who sported more medallions than hair; a blue-haired dowager drinking chartreuse from a snifter; a set of identically dressed identical twins, used-car-salesman variety; and the big winner, a flabby-armed brunette in a sleeveless dress who was a dead ringer for Bob Hope.

"When did all this happen?" Micah asked.

"The changing of the guard generally takes place around one," Barbara said.

"Every night?"

"Mm-hm."

"I didn't know you had legalized gambling in Thailand."

"We haven't."

"Do the police know about this place?"

"Of course. It's not exactly tucked away in a corner."

"Don't they object?"

She smiled. "Check out the clientele."

It was then that Micah noticed. About half the people in the room were Thai, but that half was the staff. The customers were ninety-nine-and-fourty-four-one-hundredths percent occidental.

"Tourists," he said.

Barbara laughed throatily. "Rudyard's does more business than the Grand Palace and the Temple of the Emerald Buddha combined. And pays more than its share of taxes."

The perfect front, Sinclair mused. A blatantly illegal but essentially respectable and harmless racket covering up a dead multimillion-dollar operation. From the ridiculous to the sublime.

"This way," Barbara said.

She led them past several rows of rectangular tables to a far corner near the kitchen. To a dark cloakroom. She flicked on the light switch. There was a metal door in the corner. A metal door in the farthest corner of the cloakroom in the farthest corner of the restaurant.

To the right of the metal door was a much smaller metal door. Behind it the main switches. Barbara pulled its ring handle and it opened. No, not the main switches. A bunch of numbered buttons. Like an oversized push-button phone.

She punched several numbered buttons, and the large metal door slid open. Darkness. She walked forward. Micah and Sinclair followed. A foot in front of them the walls on either side lit up.

It was a narrow passageway. As they walked forward panels of light appeared ahead on either side and went out as they were passed. Like chasing Tinkerbell.

They reached the end of the passageway after a minute or so of walking. They were in a large open space—the air gave that away—but there was very little light. Just a dangling light bulb ten feet away.

Barbara walked to the light bulb.

"Juan!" she called.

Her voice echoed.

No answer.

Sinclair and Micah both reached for their guns.

"Juan! It's Barbara," she called, even louder.

The entire room was suddenly flooded with light. Barbara gasped. Then, seeming to recognize her surroundings, she sighed with relief.

She looked at Micah and Sinclair uncertainly. "The watchman must have heard me and turned on the lights." She smiled weakly. Even she didn't believe it. "He doesn't like to be bothered with people."

Micah looked at Sinclair. "Trap?"

"No question. But forewarned . . ." He felt the cold steel in his pocket.

Micah nodded.

Barbara was in the center of the room. It was

high-ceilinged, with myriad articles lining the four walls.

There were crates, suits of armor, a piano, paintings, mannequins, rubber imitations of medieval weapons, racks of costumes, a large stuffed tiger, statues, wall hangings, knickknacks.

"Props," Barbara said inanely. Anything to break the leaden silence.

"I thought it was a garage sale," Sinclair said quietly. "Where's Jez?"

She laughed nervously and began walking backward until she ran into a large desk. Recognizing it by touch, she improvised. "This is my favorite piece," she chattered, edging to her right. "The president's desk from the first three Circle of Eight adventures." It was large and oaken, flanked by two tall flagpoles. Behind it a wide, white-leather swivel chair faced the wall.

She worked her way right some more, stopping to play idly on the out-of-tune piano. "From the waterfront-bar scene in episode two," she informed them, wide-eyed.

"Thanks for the guided tour," Micah said, tapping the trigger of his concealed .38.

All three of them knew she was going to run any second. The target looked to be a dark hole, maybe an exit, a foot or two beyond the piano.

A brief exchange of glances among all three, then it happened. Barbara ran, Sinclair and Micah aimed their pistols, and the hole was plugged by a goon in a black dinner jacket, all in a matter of seconds.

"What do you get when you cross a penguin and an ape," Micah said.

"Stalemate," Sinclair said.

Then suddenly there were three goons—then five, then ten, then more than they could count.

"Correction, Mr. Sinclair," came a famaliar voice from behind the desk. "Checkmate."

The white swivel chair spun creakily around, and Sinclair was face-to-face with D'Arbanville. "Do not even entertain the possibility of employing your weapons. The result would be irreversibly disastrous for Miss Cooke."

His wavy silver hair caught the light. He was darkly tanned. His brown eyes were wide apart, deeply placed in the skull. He sat utterly still. His face wore a sanguine smile. Framed by the white leather of the chair, he possessed the eerie flawlessness of a body in an open casket.

The adversaries locked eyes instantly. No one else in the room dared move or speak.

At length, D'Arbanville broke the silence. "A long-awaited reunion," he said mirthlessly.

He raised a finger, and goon number one shoved Barbara roughly into the center of the room. She landed on her hands and knees and stayed that way.

D'Arbanville placed his manicured hands on the desk, and Sinclair got his first look at the ring. The blue diamond eyes shone like tiny beacons.

D'Arbanville rose slowly from the chair and tugged at the cuffs of his pink silk shirt. The legion of goons turned to face him, at attention. He ignored them, more interested in the way his black tailored suit hung on his lean, muscled frame.

After adjusting the knot of his blood-red tie, chosen for Sinclair's benefit—he walked to the center of the room and stopped directly in front of the cowering Barbara. Multiple pairs of obedient eyes followed.

Barbara looked meekly up at the impassive face of her superior. "You see, Lord D'Arbanville, Juan was wrong to doubt my loyalty." Her voice was a childlike whisper. Micah felt a sudden ugly chill. "I have led the enemies directly into your trap."

It was a good try, but not good enough. D'Arbanville took hold of the back of her head firmly and pressed it against his crotch. He stroked her long black hair tenderly. "Barbara, Barbara. If only I could believe you."

"Oh, you can, Lord D'Arbanville, you can," she whispered desperately.

"No, no," he said wistfully. "You are a delicate sailboat, drifting wherever the winds of opportunity take you. Your loyalty is as palpable and consistent as that wind."

She began to sob softly.

"Please don't cry, my dear," he said gently. "It is very unbecoming. Since you have demonstrated your remorse so touchingly, I am willing to give you another chance."

She collapsed against him with relief.

Prematurely.

"After a slight chastisement. Stand up."

She did so, wiping tears and mascara from her cheeks.

He ripped the shoulder of her blouse, exposing smooth perfect skin. She gasped, her eyes widening in shock and terror.

He fished in his pocket for a minute, pulling out a small white jar. He held it up between his thumb and index finger, as if displaying it for all to see.

Waves of pure loathing overcame Sinclair as he remembered the words of Richie, the punk gang leader from the Rankamheng Bar: "He rubs the ring in this little jar he always carries, then he gives you the mark."

That's exactly what D'Arbanville did. "Consider this a birthmark, my dear. You are one of us now."

When she saw what was coming, Barbara closed her eyes tightly but didn't back away. He pressed the snake's head against the tender flesh of her shoulder. .

Her scream was bloodcurdling, more animal than human. Several of the goons winced, but no one made a move to help her.

D'Arbanville lifted the ring from her shoulder, and the screaming stopped. She breathed deeply a few times, then opened her eyes. They were dull and glassy.

The dead eyes of the snake, Sinclair thought.

Taking his time, D'Arbanville screwed the lid on the tiny white jar and dropped it back into his pocket.

He bent over and kissed her lingeringly on the mouth, then on the earlobe; then he whispered something only she could hear.

She smiled faintly.

"Now Barbara, my dear," he said, for all ears, "relieve the gentlemen of their weapons and come sit with me." He returned to the desk and settled himself into his white leather throne, silver hair spread out against the chair back like a mane.

Barbara walked mechanically, deliberately, over to Micah and stood in front of him.

An automaton, Sinclair thought.

She looked Micah straight in the eyes as she took his gun. There wasn't a trace of warmth, let alone recognition, in their black depths. Only coldness and determination.

Not an automaton. A Hitler Youth.

The look was repeated with Sinclair. Instead of letting her take his gun, however, he pressed it into her hand, squeezing hard.

She made no sound or motion that D'Arbanville could see, but her jaw tightened and she broke the stare, looking down instead.

Sinclair had to admire her resilency. Roll with the punches, Barbara.

Then the same mechanical, deliberate walk, back to D'Arbanville. She dropped the guns on the desk and sat on the chair arm, draping herself decorously.

D'Arbanville stroked and petted her as he talked. "Now that we're all comfortable . . ."

"Where's Jez?" Micah demanded.

D'Arbanville rubbed his forehead in annoyance. "Mr. Sinclair, your partner's manners are really quite abominable. Miss Cooke is safe for the time being in another quadrant of the building. You know, I really should have chilled some champagne for this occasion. I—"

"When do we get to see her?"

More forehead rubbing. "When I say so."

Good, Sinclair thought. Keep it going, hotshot.

"How do we know she isn't dead already?"

"I guess you'll just have to take my word for it." D'Arbanville's voice was getting edgier. "You haven't any other choice now, have you? Mr. Sin—"

"You make me sick."

"The feeling is unmistakably and wholeheartedly mutual." Almost an eruption.

You've got him near the edge, Sinclair thought. Just one more shove.

"You'll never get away with this," Micah threatened, shaking his fist angrily.

"I already have," D'Arbanville responded just as angrily, slamming his fist on the desk top.

Jackpot, Sinclair thought. Here comes the whole explanation. Straight from the horse's ass's mouth. Nice going, partner.

D'Arbanville gripped the arms of the chair so hard the color of his knuckles matched that of the chair. His speech was clipped and rhythmic. He spoke directly to Micah. "In one hour you will be dead, Mr. Sinclair will be dead, the lonely, inquisitive Miss Cooke will be dead. I will be in the first-class compartment of a jetliner bound for Amsterdam. Our latest shipment of cocaine, safely and innocently ensconced in film cans also containing Dreamscape's latest martial-arts epic, will be on its way to our regional representatives all over the world."

"Projectionists," Sinclair said.

"Ah, I see that the late Ms. Phillips was able to assist you in figuring out my method of transport before I sent her to greener pastures. Yes, subliminal images. Ingenious, don't you agree?"

"Very," Sinclair said.

"But not foolproof," Micah challenged.

D'Arbanville stood up. He spoke to Sinclair. "I had intended to take both of you with me to join Miss Cooke, but I'm afraid I can't bear the sight of your associate a moment longer."

He lifted Micah's gun from the desk in front of him. Holding it distastefully between two fingers like a dead rat, he dropped it into Barbara's waiting palm. "Watch the Boy Wonder. If he moves, kill him."

He turned to Sinclair. "Come with me."

chapter 20

D'Arbanville led him into a corridor that was unlike the passage Barbara had taken them through.
There was absolutely no light and no sound.

Through his shoes, Sinclair could feel a vibration,
like that of machinery in a soundproof room.

Was Jez in that room as well?

His foot hit a step, and he pitched forward, catching himself. D'Arbanville's chuckle floated down,
amused and confident.

"Do watch your step, Mr. Sinclair. Can't have
you breaking your neck, can we?"

Directed by the sound of that mocking voice,
Sinclair hurtled forward like a missile seeking its
target.

D'Arbanville uttered a short gasp; his neck was
being induced to part company with the rest of his
spinal column.

Sinclair's laugh was a roar in his ears. "You've
gotten soft, D'Arbanville. Now . . . what was that
about breaking necks?"

D'Arbanville was unperturbed. "Think, Sinclair,

how anxious my subordinates will get in my
absence. Think of poor, lovely, doomed Miss Cooke.
Should anything happen to me, they will kill her,
and so unimaginatively."

Regretfully, Sinclair loosened his hold. He could
hear the rustle of silk as D'Arbanville neatened his
mussed collar.

"You always were a reasonable man." Those
honeyed tones went on maddeningly. "How unfortunate you allowed yourself to be hampered by the
dictates of the law. I wonder why you made that
particular decision."

"Not partial to working with scum, I guess."

The stairs went on forever, it seemed. They snaked
around like the steps to the Statue of Liberty's
crown or the top bleachers at Shea. Definitely more
like Shea. A stadium. An arena.

A pit.

A door was thrust open, emitting such a blinding,
white light that Sinclair had to cover his eyes with
both hands.

As he stood there, blinking, he was roughly
thrown into the light of that new place.

Slowly, his eyes adjusted. He saw D'Arbanville
drawing off a pair of sunglasses; heaven forbid he
should be uncomfortable, even for a moment, Sinclair thought wryly.

He was flanked on either side by two muscular-
looking Asians, both armed. That mechanical vibration was now present as a rumble: the magnifi-
cation of a hungry stomach. It annoyed Sinclair;
he had a feeling he should be able to recognize the
sound but could not.

Lounging next to D'Arbanville was Lt. Valjenos;
Sinclair knew him from the Librarian's mug shot.

He looked decidedly sulky. Even in his fit of pique, Valjenos managed to ape D'Arbanville's stance and composure. When I grow up, I want to be just like you, Daddy.

"Lovely, isn't it?" His lordship gestured expansively. They were on what looked like an observation deck, all painted an antiseptic white. Sinclair wondered about this ivory mania, remembering D'Arbanville's throne in the other room.

"Expensive," he went on, motioning Sinclair to the large windows. "But well worth it, don't you think?"

Slowly, Sinclair went to the window. Whatever hungry machine was making that rumble was down there.

Valjenos began to laugh. He didn't have D'Arbanville's lord-of-the-manor bass down pat; hyena hysteria was the best he could do.

From the window, Sinclair saw a flagpole. Nothing frightening there, just a flagpole, no flag. He took a step closer. From the flagpole issued a rope. A nice, stout rope. That was all right, too.

He took a deep breath, grabbed the railing, hauled himself right up to the glass.

From the rope, her wrists lashed together, one drop of blood streaking down her innocent arm, was Jezebel, suspended over a dead-white pit. In all that stark blankness, that one drop, was very clear, and very red.

And he knew what the rumble was, now.

"We used them in the first Circle of Eight film," D'Arbanville explained. "After that, we simply could not part with them. Very useful they are, and rather endearing, as you can see for yourself.

Numb, Sinclair forced himself to look at the

restless bodies in the pit, not too far below Jez's toes. They were pretty, really; Sinclair loved the grace of the big cats, and these black leopards were exceptionally beautiful.

The drop of blood ski-jumped off Jez's elbow and fell into the pit. The leopards growled hungrily.

"Poor things," D'Arbanville said with real emotion. "They haven't had anything to eat since Sammy, and he was weeks ago."

Valjenos continued to stare moodily at Jez. He did not want the leopards to eat her. He wanted her all to himself. When he was boss someday . . . He watched the leopards and sympathized. D'Arbanville starved them all.

Through the glass, Jez found Sinclair's eyes. She was past fear and into resignation.

Amanda had worn that same look into eternity.

"It's the old shell game, Steve," D'Arbanville whispered. Pleased, he stared into the depths of the serpent's cold diamond eyes. It had advised him well. "I had you then, and I have you now."

*   *   *

Even while clutching his gun in her manicured hands, Micah found Barbara charming. Of course, the serpent's head brand on her shoulder spoiled the effect.

Actually, Micah frowned, the fact that she was holding that gun on him really blew the picture.

"Oh, Barbara." He sighed. "Barbara, Barbara, Barbara. What a disappointment you've been."

"What am I supposed to do?" she snarled. Her shoulder smarted dreadfully. "Rot in jail for the rest of my life?"

He watched her. "I would never have turned you in, Barbara. I liked you."

"Sure." She laughed shortly. The thugs behind her plastered elaborately unlistening looks on their faces.

"You could have been a contender, Barbara, instead of . . . the poor, wounded butterfly you are."

"Huh." She dropped her voice. "I told you, I'm very expensive. You could never take care of me."

"Maybe not." His eyes slid to the angry wound on her shoulder. "But I would never have done that to you."

The next thing that happened was poetry, absolute Shakespeare.

He launched himself into the air just as Barbara brought the barrel of the .38 in line with D'Arbanville's number-one goon. The thug never had a chance to use his submachine gun. She plugged him squarely between the eyes, then wrenched the rifle from his dying grasp.

Micah heard her start to mow them down as he dove behind the white elephant chair. A stray shot dug into the chair; groaning, it bled stuffing. Seconds later, Barbara joined him under the desk, pegging shots at anyone who came close. She tossed him a small pistol.

"I am no longer disappointed in you," Micah said. The thugs had pushed down a costume rack and, hiding behind the bright silks and masks, were encroaching on the desk stronghold. Micah saw a hand paddling between a blue chiffon and a gorilla suit and took careful aim. After a healthy scream, a man fell back, nursing a bleeding thumb. The wounded man tried a left-handed shot, ruffling Barbara's hair. She clipped him in the knee to discourage any further bright ideas.

"I figure . . ." she said slowly, following the progress of the costume rack, "being such a cooperative person, perhaps I could get off with a suspended sentence."

Micah kept a close watch on the gorilla's head. Were the eyes shining a little more than they should be?

Barbara nudged him. "What about it?"

"Uhhh, I can't promise anything, but definitely a reduced sentence."

She shot the nose off the gorilla. "Not good enough."

"You could view it as a vacation! Was the desk chair starting to move? "You could learn a new trade." A hand appeared over the chair. Micah waited for the head and shoulders and blasted away.

He looked at the pistol, chagrinned. It was empty. "Damn Derringer."

Barbara jerked her head toward the door. "Run for it; I'll cover you." He looked at her doubtfully. "Trust me." She smiled wickedly.

He raced for the door, hearing a particularly fierce scream behind him. At first he thought it was the rest of the gorilla gone to its final reward, but it was just Barbara screaming every choice Thai curse she knew.

When he hit the corridor, she'd started on her Chinese profanity. He didn't think the thugs stood a chance.

The corridor was dark, holding no clue as to which direction D'Arbanville had led Sinclair. He leaned against the wall, trying to get his bearings, and felt a door at his back.

He pushed at it. It gave slightly and then caught; like a heavy weight was shored up against the other side of the door. For a second, his mind conjured up a grisly picture of Jez's body, thrown carelessly up against the door, limbs at an impossible angle.

It couldn't be, she couldn't be dead.

He pulled the door back toward him, then pushed hard. The obstacle gave and he fell forward . . . into a pit full of black leopards. The door behind him locked malevolently.

The last animal Micah had tried to hypnotize had been a senile tomcat with the nasty habit of shitting on the bathtub drain. House cats, leopards. Same thing only bigger, a little more energy.

He concentrated. Growls became purrs, angry pacing turned to graceful lounging.

A drop of blood spattered onto his hand. His concentration broke, and it took a real effort to reestablish control. Above him, Jez dangled from a rope. At least she wasn't dead. Yet.

He saw her dip her head, a flicker of recognition in her eyes. Then she straightened, staring off at something he could not see, because of the overhang running around the pit.

He had a pretty good idea what was up there, anyway. Well, if he couldn't see them, it followed they couldn't see him.

Sweat began to trickle down his forehead. He hoped they'd cut her down soon; he couldn't hold the leopards forever. He'd grab Jez and run; Sinclair would have to look after himself.

In the observation deck, Sinclair caught something no one else seemed to take notice of. He heard the growls of the big cats diminish.

D'Arbanville continued to hold forth on how smart he was. The leopards now sounded as if they'd all decided to go out for a Big Mac and forget about the Jezburgers.

The lady in question looked first at Sinclair, then down into the pit. He was tempted to crack a smile; the shell game wasn't over by a long shot.

Valjenos caught his expression but not its significance. He's losing it, the lieutenant thought. Not such a tough guy after all, and the boss so scared of him. When I'm boss . . ."

"Chee," D'Arbanville nodded to one of the orientals guarding Sinclair. "Feed the leopards." He caressed the coiled serpent resting on his hand.

Chee unlocked one of the huge window panels, pulling a long knife out of his jacket. He shinnied out onto the flagpole, knife clutched in his teeth like a pirate.

Jez began to swing back and forth, as Chee's considerable weight influenced the flagpole.

Down in the pit, Micah felt a nerve twitching under his left eye. Hurry.

Suddenly Chee tried to sit bolt upright on the flagpole. Jez's body began to jerk on the line like a hooked fish.

Sinclair froze, paralyzed. None of them could see what had really happened.

The delight of Chee's life was his beautiful wrist chronometer, capable of computing a moon shot all by itself. It was a bulky, clumsy thing.

It was caught on the pole.

"This is madness," D'Arbanville said, turning to his lieutenant. "Shoot her."

"What a waste," Valjenos muttered.

D'Arbanville shot him a stern look. Reluctantly, Valjenos went for his gun.

That reluctance bought the extra seconds Sinclair needed. He plowed into Valjenos, hearing the report of the gun as they both fell to the ground.

On the pole, Chee clutched his chest and breathed his last. He toppled, his body describing a short arc; his snarled wristwatch remained trapped on the line.

A second later, the rope snapped and Jez plummeted into the pit.

Valjenos had the breath knocked out of him. Ling, the second bodyguard, was going for his jacket pocket. Probably not for ID, Sinclair reasoned, grabbing the fallen lieutenant's gun.

He shot Ling through the heart; a clean, fast kill, the man's astonished expression told him.

Valjenos was staying down. D'Arbanville? Gone, slipped out at the first opportune moment. But not forgotten, Sinclair thought grimly.

He peered over the edge of the pit. Jez was lying flat on her back, a leopard docilely licking the raw wounds on her wrist.

"Jez?" He called down.

"Right here." She was watching that leopard nervously. "So's the whiz kid, doing his Svengali bit."

"I know. You okay?"

"Confused, but breathing."

Sinclair threw a look over his shoulder. "So's Valjenos."

Jez's eyes glittered. "Leave him for me. Get D'Arbanville."

"You bet, lady."

She heard the echo of his racing steps.

Jez stood; she could just touch Chee's foot. The leopard was now sucking on her toes. Jez pulled herself over Chee's body and headed for the deck. Her face was serene.

"Hon?" Micah called from his corner. "Please hurry, the guests are getting hungry and we're running out of Cheez-Whiz and crackers." His eyes were beginning to glaze over.

When Jez reached the deck, Valjenos was on his feet waiting for her. He met her at the railing.

"You killed her, didn't you?"

Valjenos nodded.

"And Sammy."

His lips split in a grin. "She killed Sammy."

"Tina?"

"Little American bitch." He began to laugh, shoulders shaking helplessly. The cosmic joke of all time: timid, gentle Tina turned murderess.

Jez never felt her own motion, she merely observed her body advancing through the air, arms outstretched in a horrible parody of a lover's embrace. With that same detached air, she saw her hands snake around his neck and fasten there as his did around hers. She was not aware of the pressure around her throat, only of the strength in her own arms.

Valjenos's face lost its amused air; his eyes started to bug out. He looked a little surprised, then very surprised, then inspired.

Twisting his body, he sent them both crashing down into the pit.

"Jez? Jez, are you all right?" Micah was pulling her off Valjenos's body. His back had been broken when she'd fallen on him. His eyes were closed.

"I got him," Jez whispered incredulously. "I really got him."

"That's right." Micah put his arm around her.

They were surrounded by the leopards, just beginning to shake off their stupor. "And now they have us."

Valjenos's eyes rolled open. He moaned. "I can't move." He caught sight of the big cats. Tears began to roll down his cheeks.

"Time to leave," Jez said. She yanked at the pit door behind them. It held fast. "It's stuck! Give me a hand."

Valjenos had struck up an unnatural keening, like a banshee. The leopards were intrigued.

"Jez." Micah gently pried her fingers from the doorknob. "It's locked."

She stopped struggling. "Oh, God, this is it."

He looked at her. "Probably."

"Oh, hell." She kissed him. He kissed back. The leopards' growls were beginning to drown out Valjenos's wails.

The pit door was flung open, scattering leopards and lovers alike.

"A one-track mind," Barbara observed. In one hand, she grasped a ring of keys any concierge would be proud of.

"Barbara, I could kiss you," Micah yelled enthusiastically.

"Should I get in line?" She tried to close the door behind them and nearly got knocked over by a leopard deluge.

"Help me!" She screamed. Leopards were loping down the corridor, chasing the tantalizing scent of Rudyard's New York cut.

Micah bashed a leopard on its nose, sending it back into the pit, all alone with Valjenos. It was hungry. It was in a rotten mood.

Valjenos began to scream. "You can't leave me. You can't."

"You bastard!" Barbara howled, slamming the door on him.

Micah leaned against the wall, listening to the sweat dry on his skin. Anything was better than listening to Valjenos and the leopard.

"Please—please—please—I'll be good, I'll do anything you say, only don't . . ."

The leopard made no such promises.

After a while, all they heard was the leopard eating.

chapter 21

Sinclair backtracked as quickly as he could. First down the long spiral of stairs, then through the pitch-dark passage where D'Arbanville had led him.

Only it wasn't so dark this time. A rectangular light shone at the end, illuminating some of the passage, beckoning.

Had D'Arbanville left the door open in his haste to escape? Or as a trap? Sinclair didn't stop to ponder. He raced to the light.

It came from the big storage room, site of the goon convention and Barbara's baptism. The place was littered with corpses. D'Arbanville's white swivel throne squeaked spastically like a just-abandoned hobbyhorse. Sinclair glanced over the bodies briefly. No dragonlady. Hm.

There was a flicker of movement to the left. Something black.

It popped up suddenly, like a jack-in-the-box. A splash of red on black. D'Arbanville's red tie. Sinclair dived behind the piano, just avoiding the two sharp pings that followed. They made small holes in the wall beside him.

A clicking sound. Another. The sound of metal hitting concrete. A whiff of cologne, sickly sweet. Footsteps, running.

He looked up. D'Arbanville was heading for the lighted passage, the one leading to the casino.

You'll never get away, slime, Sinclair thought. Not this time. He felt a sudden surge of adrenaline. It pumped through his body, feeding his rage, magnifying his long-suppressed desire for revenge.

Stepping over bodies, throwing aside everything in his path, he raced to get hold of D'Arbanville.

The illuminating panels flickered on-off on-off faster than a strobe light as he ran, hell-bent, down the passageway.

D'Arbanville was at the big metal door, frantically pushing buttons on a console identical to the one Barbara had manipulated so coolly on the other side. Sinclair reached him just as the metal door slid noisily open.

D'Arbanville was halfway through the opening when Sinclair caught hold of his black collar and yanked. A jolt like an electric shock went through his body, and he was jerked backward as if weightless.

Sinclair spun him around and started to work him over. He used quick rabbit punches. Painful, but not nearly powerful enough to send him into unconsciousness. That was the last thing Sinclair wanted.

When he saw that D'Arbanville was starting to fade, Sinclair spun him back around and threw him headlong through the doorway into the small cloakroom.

Lord D'Arbanville landed in a heap, like a rag doll. But the crime czar was nothing if not resourceful. He shook his head once, twice, to clear it, then reached desperately for the nearest object.

It was a standing metal ashtray, three feet high. He clutched it with two hands like a barbell, then threw it forward with all his might.

It hit Sinclair in the shoulder, and he was knocked momentarily off balance. D'Arbanville managed to get to his feet and stagger out of the cloakroom before Sinclair hurled the ashtray effortlessly through the nearest wall and resumed chase.

If anything, Rudyard's was more packed with gamblers than it had been an hour ago on Sinclair's first trip through.

D'Arbanville's forward progress through the casino was slow and unsteady, due to the crowd and his spinning head. Patrons assumed he was a drunk looking for a vomitorium and ignored him. He threw everything he could get his hands on into Sinclair's path, in a vain attempt to stop, or at least delay, what he knew was coming.

Sinclair stalked him unhurriedly. His eyes were gray bullets. His fist rhythmically pounded his palm and every red table that he passed.

The gap between the two men gradually narrowed.

Sinclair caught up with him near the black octagon in the center of the room. Running out of objects, D'Arbanville grabbed the cotton-candy blond roughly by the arm. He intended to use her as a human wedge, but her bald friend had something to say about it. They played tug-o-war with her for a while, until she complained nasally, "What do you think I am, anyway? A wishbone? Leggo!"

Sinclair, meanwhile, had closed the gap completely. He grabbed a handful of D'Arbanville's silver hair and threw him, screaming, against the octagon.

A considerable disruption among the players at the star table resulted.

"Harvey, I'm getting my stole," the cotton-candy blond screamed through pink lips. "Bring the car around." She wiggled away in the direction of the cloakroom.

Harvey/baldy started for the front door.

The wet-headed Latin used the opportunity to minimize his losses by pocketing Harvey's abandoned chips. He swaggered nonchalantly to the cash-in window.

Bob Hope likewise began scooping up whatever chips she could lay her hands on. She scanned the casino for another game and, spotting what looked like a table of suckers, sidled over and joined them.

The identical twins backed up a step or two to watch.

The blue-haired dowager polished off her snifter of chartreuse, then didn't move a muscle.

The dealer vaulted from the tiny center hole over the side of the octagon to safety. She looked around for a bouncer to break up the fight, but there didn't seem to be any.

Sinclair's left hand still gripped D'Arbanville's silver mane, his right was clamped over the silk-covered throat. He spoke in a whisper. "I could never hurt you enough to even the score." He gripped the throat more tightly. D'Arbanville gasped. "But I'm sincerely going to try."

*   *   *

Lights flickered on and off in the Tinkerbell passage as they ran past; Barbara leading, Micah and Jez pumping along behind her.

Suddenly Barbara skidded to a stop.

"What is it?" Jez called out. She was in no mood to play any more of Dreamscape's party games. Micah held up a restraining hand, waiting for Barbara's report. After the scene with the leopards, his radar was on the fritz and probably would be for the next twelve hours. Completely out of Cheez-Whiz and crackers. Old Mother Hubbard and her dog would have starved on the contents of his mental cupboard.

Jez was done in, too. When it came to facing certain death, three times a day seemed to be her limit.

Barbara turned around slowly. She had Micah's .38 in her hand. Her expression was pleasant, slightly formal. "I suppose this calls for an explanation," she said, aiming at Micah. Jez considered rushing her but dismissed the idea, too risky. Barbara'd still shoot Micah and then probably be a little peeved at Jez for making her rush her shot.

"I'm listening, Barbara," Micah said quietly.

"I thought my cooperation would buy you off. A little late in the game for my redemption, it seems. I will not go to jail."

"I said I would do everything I could."

She smiled. "Do you remember what I said? Not good enough," She took a step back. Jez saw a slight unevenness in the floor; she hoped Barbara would stumble, but her step was sure. Barbara Tiang had already made all the mistakes she intended to.

Micah frowned. "Barbara, shooting the good guys does not exactly qualify you for Miss Congeniality."

"Such a diplomat." She turned to Jez. "Is he always like that?"

Jez shrugged helplessly. This reminded her of the time she'd been at the senior prom with her best friend's guy. That time she'd wound up with her face in the punch bowl, followed by a girl's room brawl. Jez had won that battle. Somehow she didn't think Barbara would go for that solution and Jez didn't see a girls' room around anywhere.

"I'm a survivor, Michael . . . if that is your name."

"Close enough."

"Doesn't matter now." She smiled sadly. "I'm afraid I've played dumb with you. I know all about Puccini and his Madame Butterfly. She killed herself for the man she loved. I don't suppose I'll ever love any man more than life itself, but I did like you." She drew a bead on his forehead. "Enough to run away with you. Too bad we're on opposite sides, too bad I didn't meet you a long time ago . . ." She looked at Jez, annoyed. "Too bad you didn't leave her home."

"Barbara . . ."

"No, no more talk. Will you turn your back and let me walk away?"

He held out his hands. "I can't."

She sighed thoughtfully. "Then we have a problem." She pulled the trigger.

Given the range she was at and the shape of the corridor, the blast was incedibly loud. The second after the bang hit her ears, Jez felt a scream bypass her brain and head directly for her throat. It echoed, loud and familiar . . . yup, that's me screaming, all right.

She saw Micah fly back against the wall, like a giant hand had slammed into him.

"Sorry," Barbara said with genuine regret and started hightailing it down the corridor, lights flashing as she went.

"You . . . tramp!" Jez screamed. She heard a low chuckle from the floor. "Thank God, you're not dead."

"Tramp?" Micah looked up at her. "I don't know, Jez; you think that was a little strong?" He was holding on to his right shoulder; blood was seeping steadily through his fingers. His face had taken on a shiny pallor.

Jez didn't feel very well herself. She had a little first-aid pamphlet back in her apartment, but all she'd ever read in it were "eye infections" and "stab wounds." "Stab wounds" were probably more applicable in this case than "eye infections," and all she could remember of that chapter was something about traumatic shock.

"Are you in shock?" she asked. him..

"Yeah." Micah nodded. "I never thought she'd shoot." He looked at Jez's green face. "Would you relax? It's not that bad; I think it went right through."

Jez grimaced. "That makes me feel a whole lot better. This is the first time I saw a friend get shot."

"Well, this is the first time I've been shot, so we're even. What are you doing?"

She was trying to rip his sleeve off. "Making you a bandage."

He watched her, frowning. "If you were really my friend, you'd rip up your own clothes."

She hunkered over him, ripping the thin material with her teeth so she could tie the mess together. She eyed the bandage critically. Not the kind of job that would earn a Girl Scout a merit badge, but it was holding. "Can you stand?"

He thought about it. "Nope."

"Don't be a baby, come on." She grabbed his right arm.

"Not that arm! Not that arm!"

"All right, I heard you!" She managed to get him on his feet, his left arm draped cozily over her shoulders, her arm wrapped around his waist. They tried a step forward in tandem, but as Micah's weight swung forward, he threw Jez off balance. They crashed back into the wall.

"Yeow!"

"Sorry."

They lurched forward, a little more balanced this time.

"I hope Barbara gets away clean," Micah said, surprising the hell out of Jez.

She noticed her bandage wasn't doing much good; it was soaked through. He had to be feeling pretty lousy.

"I think she'd be okay if she could just get a second chance," he explained, flashing Jez a smile of pure warmth and charm. "I'm a great believer in second chances. Ain't you, Cookie?"

She thought about Beautiful Universe, a million light-years away in Pluto's voting district. What do you want to be when you grow up, Jezebel? Oh, I don't know, I think I'll be a secret agent, fight for truth, justice, and . . . second chances. She got a firmer hold on Micah's waist and charged him with a little charisma of her own. "You bet I do, partner."

They weren't moving fast, but they were definitely getting out of there with a modicum of dignity.

Not too shabby.

chapter 22

Sinclair couldn't hit him often enough, hard enough. Couldn't stop hitting him.

D'Arbanville's face had started to take on the color and texture of raw hamburger. Bloodstains dotted his clothes. His body was limp and lifeless. But his eyes. His eyes wouldn't surrender. They stared coldly into Sinclair's, challenging, daring him. If you can dish it out, I can take it. And when you're tired of beating on me, and you think you've won, and you let me go, then the snake will strike.

"Hit him again, honey," the dowager slurred drunkenly, waving her glass. "Smug bastard. Look at that smarmy face. Not even a mother could love it."

Sinclair picked up a glass of water and tossed its contents into D'Arbanville's leering face. He spluttered involuntarily, and a glimmer of rage flared up in the brown eyes. Then the cold stare returned, more riveting and determinded than before.

"Thass a way, baby. Thass—"

The dowager's cheerleading was cut short by

a high-pitched scream, of the lady-in-distress variety.

All activity in the room abruptly stopped. Everyone looked around in alarm and confusion.

A second later, the cotton-candy blond came running out of the cloakroom, screaming hysterically.

The clientele or Rudyard's breathed a collective sigh. Nothing to worry about. Just the flaky blond. Let's get back to the game.

Then three black leopards strolled in.

Nobody noticed at first. The curious ones, who hadn't gone back to their games, were watching the blond, not the cloakroom.

"But, Harvey, but Harvey," she was shrilly protesting, as baldy led her out the front door.

One of the leopards held a mink stole in his teeth, proudly displaying it like a prize kill. The other two were calmly strolling around the casino, in search of prizes of their own.

The one with the mink bumped into a table. A man in a checked shirt looked up, blinked, looked again, and let out a scream to rival the blond's.

It wasn't long before most of Rudyard's was screaming and making tracks for the exit. A huge bottleneck resulted. People in the rear of the mob tried to throw themselves over the top of the crowd like quarterbacks straining for extra yardage.

The dowager was nonplussed. "Who let the cat out of the bag?" she demanded surlily, helping herself to the chartruese bottle.

Sinclair grabbed D'Arbanville by the lapels and hoisted him up onto the octagon. "Sit tight," he said, and pushed. D'Arbanville fell back onto the black velvet surface as onto a bed. He lay motionless on his back, semiconsciously watching the crystal chandelier twinkle above him.

Sinclair assumed that Micah was behind the leopard brigade. He looked around the emptying casino. No sign of hotshot, or Jez.

The leopards seemed to be more curious than predatory. One of them was stretching out near the bar. He gave a loud yawn-growl and dropped his head onto his paws. Maybe they've already pigged out and are just looking for a motel, Sinclair mused.

The one with the mink was also settling down. He'd amassed a large quantity of chips and, mink stole beneath him like a bearskin rug, was curling up contentedly with his spoils.

The third leopard, considerably heftier and more finicky than his friends, was still prowling Rudyard's for a place to hang his hat.

The screaming of the customers shoving to get out made him edgy, and he roared several times in annoyance. This only caused the screaming to increase, which caused the roaring to increase, which . . .

The shimmering chandelier caught his eye, and he stalked in an ever-tightening circle closer and closer to the octagon that rested underneath it.

Sinclair was so engrossed in the ritual of the leopard that he didn't notice the appearance of Micah and Jez until they were next to him.

"What's she doing?" Jez asked.

"He," Sinclair said, "is staking out a resting place." He turned to Micah, noticed his bleeding arm and the way he was hanging on to Jez. "What happened to you?"

"Cleaning my gun."

In two smooth movements, the leopard went from the ground to the top of the octagon and onto the chandelier. He swung contentedly like a child on a rope.

D'Arbanville looked up terrified. He began making incoherent sounds, little whimpers and groans. His body tensed as if trying to move, but he didn't have the strength.

The chandelier was clearly unable to bear the weight of the big cat. It rumbled ominously, plaster falling from the ceiling onto the helpless D'Arbanville.

The dowager laughed, a long cackle, and the chandelier came crashing down, its tip skewering D'Arbanville in the stomach. Blood gushed from his belly, he screamed hideously, writhed in pain for a few seconds, and was dead.

The leopard, sullen and unnerved, leaped gracefully to the floor and padded out the front door of Rudyard's, into the dark night.

The dowager raised the chartreuse bottle. "'Twas beauty killed the beast." She cackled, and both her head and the bottle fell to the floor with a clunk.

"Don't drink to that," Sinclair said.

chapter 23

Pamela couldn't have been happier.

To begin with, the library had a new coffeemaker, very modern, very efficient. Pamela loved efficiency.

She fed water into the machine—it had already measured out the grounds for her—and punched a button. It worked like a dream; God bless progress.

With a discerning eye, she selected some very nice-looking Danish: an assortment of cheese, prune, and something that was passing for cherry. One never knew what the great man might be in the mood for.

She picked up the newspaper he'd requested and folded it neatly—a skill any paperboy would envy—and set it on her tray next to the pastry. The coffee was ready, and she poured it into a thermal pot and added that to the tray.

The machine was equipped with a carafe for boiling water, which Pamela poured into a little kettle. The tea bag was already in there, just waiting for its baptismal splash.

A small pitcher of cream and a few packets of

sugar completed the repast. Pamela glanced at her watch. A little late for high tea, but no matter.

It wasn't every day she had tea with the Librarian.

She caught herself humming, of all things, "If I Knew You Were Coming, I'd Have Baked a Cake." How silly.

He had the door open just as she reached it. He always did; she never knew exactly how, but he always did.

"Come right in, Pamela. As always, your timing is impeccable." The Librarian was his usual self; by his manner one wouldn't suspect it was a special day.

But there it was, the TV was on. Not usual at all.

She prepared his coffee—black, one sugar, while the network news wound through its lead story of murder and mayhem. She glanced at it briefly, recording in her data-bank mind the names and ages of the victims as well as the anchorman's unfortunate selection of a tie. She made herself a cup of tea, cream, no sugar; decided she was too keyed up for a Danish.

She sat back in her chair; her no-nonsense skirt riding up on those surprisingly good legs.

"How's your tea?"

"Lovely."

They spent a few companionable minutes sipping and watching.

The Librarian read the paper.

A picture of Tina Cooke flashed across the TV. Pamela leaned forward intently.

   . . .beautiful American acress Tina Cooke met a mysterious death in Thailand while on location, filming a kung-fu movie. Originally, she was implicated in a sordid web of narcotics and intrigue, but Thai police recently cleared the 26 year old actress's name, arresting the guilty parties in a raid on a local tourist attraction, Rudyard's, later discovered to be a front for illegal gambling.

The picture changed, showing an attractive man in his early sixties. His blue eyes were incredibly animated, despite his somber mood. Superimposed over his collar were the words "former Senator Toby Cooke," and underneath that, "actress's father."

"We always felt Tina was innocent." His voice was arresting. Jezebel had certainly come by her charm honestly, Pamela thought. "I like to think she rests easier now that the world knows."

Pamela clicked off the TV. She looked at the newspaper on the tray; its headline proclaiming, ACTRESS INNOCENT. In smaller letters: COCAINE BUST IN THAILAND, RINGLEADER DIES IN FREAK ACCIDENT." They ran Tina's résumé picture right on the front page; beautiful redheads made great copy.

The Librarian caught her glance and smiled. "Are you satisfied?"

"Oh, yes. Though I wish," she added wistfully, "we could have taken the credit due us. Thai police indeed."

"The Association doesn't need publicity."

"Still, it would have been nice for Miss Cooke." She stirred her tea. It didn't need it.

"Miss Cooke did turn out to be a pleasant surprise." He smiled at Pemala graciously. "You are to be congratulated. I didn't expect her to work out under fire as well as she did."

"I was very flattered you trusted my judgment. I

just had a feeling about Miss Cooke. It was Micah I was worried about." The Danish were enticing but she still felt a little nervy.

"Well, I think we found him a very nice home to grow up in." The film files were lying on his desk, the files: Sinclair, Micah, Cooke. He gestured to them casually.

"When you have a minute, file these. You can file them together. I think we can keep this team . . . busy. Oh, not right this second, Pamela." He waved her back into the chair. "We are both to be congratulated. We pulled it off . . . again."

Pamela smiled. "All three back home safely. A very successful mission."

"Very." He looked at the files nestled together.

She saluted him with her orange pekoe. "And so, it ends."

He held up his coffee cup, looking into the great unknown of its murky depths.

"So it begins."

Not for nothing was he the great man.

epilogue

Ma had to admit it, they were back and they were safe. And showing Ma's Diner a pretty lively time.

Sinclair hadn't arrived yet, but his cohorts seemed to be managing.

Linda Ronstadt was still wailing about tainted love on the juke, but she was pretty up-tempo about it. Enough so to keep that pretty Jezebel bopping with Lucille's fourteen-year-old boy. He had some fruity name—Justin, Jason, something like that. Ma thought a dumb name like that was enough cruelty to visit on a kid to keep him resentful for the rest of his life.

Maybe that's what had happened to Micah to make him so contrary. Funny thing is, he didn't seem that way anymore. He was sitting at the counter, trying to teach Ruby how to juggle; a hopeless task with one arm in a sling, but she was grinning away, basking in a little male attention. Then he said something funny and Ruby threw her head back and laughed. He watched her, enjoying her laughter, not sitting back and looking for a way to outsmart her or make her feel small.

Ma reflected. It was like sending a boy to college, and lo and behold, he comes back a man.

Lucille was keeping a maternal eye on Justin/Jason. Probably didn't want him to get overheated. Ma figured dancing with Jezebel was going to get that boy overheated for a month. Just watching was doing wonders for Ma.

Everybody'd had a few beers by now and past hurts were quickly flying out the window. Ma thought beer had it all over penicillin. Especially Budweiser.

Even Linda Ronstadt seemed to have perked up some. She was now preparing to go out and stomp all over that guy that fandangoed on her heart.

"Steve!" Jez descended on Sinclair as soon as he got through the door. "Did you see my dad on TV?"

"Sure did." Sinclair threw a friendly salute to Micah over at the counter. "Hi, partner, how's the shoulder?"

"Still there." The fruit he'd been juggling started going into business for themselves. One apple landed at Justin/Jason's feet. He ignored it and continued staring at Jez's breasts.

"I think we'd best get on home," Lucille put in. "Ruby, can you ride me and Nicholas home?"

Ma looked startled. Where the hell had he gotten Justin/Jason from?

"Sure." Ruby gathered up her stuff, handing Lucille her coat and bag.

"Come on, Nicholas."

"Good-bye, Nicky. You dance swell." Jez thought he was a nice kid.

He smiled at her shyly. If he'd had a hat he would have been twisting it in his hands. "Goodbye, Miss Cooke. You sure are pretty."

Lucille collared him and dragged him out.

Jez plopped down into a booth. "God, even the fourteen-year-olds look good to me."

Micah joined her. "You oversexed old bat."

"Who's oversexed?" She looked offended. "In the leopard pit . . ."

"What happened in the leopard pit?" Sinclair put in suspiciously.

"Mai Penrai," Micah said sweetly. "That's Thai for 'Never mind.' "

"I know what it means."

"Hm. No wonder Barbara shot you," Jez scoffed.

"You are cruel, Cookie."

"Stop calling me that!" She started to fiddle with the napkin dispenser on the table; lining it up neatly with the ketchup bottle.

"Hey!" Micah punched Sinclair's shoulder lightly. "Aren't we supposed to beat each other to a senseless pulp, or something equally intelligent?"

Sinclair nodded. "I seem to remember you making noises to that effect. However . . ." He tapped the sling one of Micah's arms was currently vacationing in.

"Oh, that," Micah said airily. "I can lick you . . ."

" . . .with one hand tied behind my back." Sinclair finished.

Jez groaned, closing her eyes. "Boys," she murmured, "you cannot be in the talent show until you get a new routine."

"I'll take a raincheck." Sinclair's eyes glinted. "But one of these days, I will collect."

Micah turned to Jez. "What about you? Wanna fight?"

She was still busy with the condiments. Salt and pepper were now lined up precisely and she was going for the little bowl of Sweet and Low. Sinclair and Micah watched her with exaggerated interest.

She looked up. "I can't help it, I love order. I'm a Libra."

"I had a friend who was very into astrology," Sinclair said softly. He smiled to himself; it suddenly occurred to him that Amanda would have liked Jez very much. "Which reminds me . . ." He dug into his pocket, spun a piece of flat plastic onto the table in front of Jez.

She picked it up. "What's this?"

"Your Association ID." Micah grinned, hanging over her shoulder. "It's official. The Librarian wants to marry you."

"Well, as we Texans say . . ." Jez looked an awful lot like Toby Cooke's wild daughter just then. "Shee-yit! Let's have some beer!"

Micah frowned, looking at Jez. "I suppose this means our wrestling match is postponed indefinitely."

"I would say so," Steve interjected drily.

"How 'bout champagne?" Ma had slipped out of the room while they were going through the first meeting of their mutual admiration society. "I had this cooling in my office." Deftly he poured and handed paper cups all around. It was either paper cups or coffee mugs. Ma liked the paper cups anyway; they had those little *Star Wars* guys on them.

"What should we drink to?" Jez asked.

They all got quiet, like kids when the campfire burns low, each wrapped in his own remembrance of their first mission.

"Old friends, new friends?"

"D'Arbanville, for bringing us together!" That was Micah. Still a smart-ass.

"Not on your perforated life," Steve retorted.

Ma coughed. "You guys open to suggestions?" He now had their attention.

They all raised their glasses to him.

"Seems to me, the world's gotten so small, most men . . . and women"—he bowed to Jez—"don't care about nothing and no one enough to die for 'em." He smiled sadly. "Maybe we're just lucky. Caring about something that much."

Sinclair laughed genially. "This is some speech, Ma."

Ma glared. "I ain't finished." He stood, waiting patiently until they all lumbered to their feet.

"To the Fail-Safe Force, long may she wave!"

They all drained their paper cups; and though the next day they all had terrible sick hangovers, they privately agreed that the champagne had to be a rare vintage.

It was really something special.